He Was All Arrogant Male.

Totally sure of himself and his impact on her. And she wished she could prove him wrong. Wished she could take a step away from him and dismiss him with a snooty comment that would put him in his place.

He smelled even better up close than he had when she'd shaken his hand. He crowded closer to her and she fought not to back up. But in the end her need for personal space won out and she inched away from him.

"You're crowding me," she said carefully. She was completely out of her element with this man.

"Good."

"Why good?"

"I like it when you get your back up."

"I don't 'get my back up.' I'm a well-bred young lady."

"I'm not a well-bred man," he said.

Dear Reader,

I've always loved romance stories that involved revenge. I think it's because I've dedicated my life to being a good girl and always fair to everyone. I like the thought of plotting revenge, and then going after it in fiction.

Gavin Renard is a man bent on revenge. The course of his life changed when he was on the cusp of adulthood. His safe, affluent family was shattered by the actions of August Lambert, and from that moment on Gavin wanted revenge.

Tempest Lambert has spent her entire life trying to get her father's attention. The heiress has done everything from being a brilliant straight-A overachiever to turning into the tabloids' favorite subject with her outrageous behavior. And through it all she's still not done more than get a raised eyebrow from her father.

But from the moment she meets Gavin she forgets about getting a reaction out of her father. Though she knows they are business rivals she falls for Gavin. Their story is one of redemption and second chances.

Please stop by my Web site at www.katherinegarbera.com for a behind-the-scenes look into *High-Society Mistress*.

Happy reading!

Katherine

KATHERINE GARBERA

HIGH-SOCIETY
MISTRESS

Published by Silhouette Books
America's Publisher of Contemporary Romance

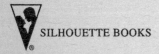

SILHOUETTE BOOKS

ISBN-13: 978-0-373-76808-0
ISBN-10:   0-373-76808-7

HIGH-SOCIETY MISTRESS

Visit Silhouette Books at www.eHarlequin.com

Printed in U.S.A.

KATHERINE GARBERA

is a strong believer in happily ever after. She found her own after meeting her Prince Charming in Fantasyland at Walt Disney World. She's written more than thirty books and has been nominated for *Romantic Times BOOKreviews* career achievement awards in Series Fantasy and Series Adventure. Katherine recently moved to the Dallas area where she lives with her husband and their two children. Visit Katherine on the Web at www.katherinegarbera.com.

This book is dedicated to all the readers at katherinegarbera.com. Thanks for always playing with me at Chatty Kathy!

One

Tempest Lambert, the tabloid's favorite party girl extraordinaire, stood quietly in the foyer of her condo building, dressed conservatively and trying not to be nervous. It was silly really. She'd charmed heads of state and celebrities. She'd made the world her oyster. But one man still had the power to reduce her to a nervous wreck.

Her father's chauffeur-driven car arrived promptly at 7:35 p.m. Tempest normally would have driven herself to the Leukemia Foundation Gala dinner and silent auction but her father had wanted to speak with her in person. And this was the only time he had in his schedule.

So here she was trying to smile and pretend that

this wasn't a big deal. And when her father didn't get out of the car to greet her she had her first inkling that it really wasn't a big deal to him.

"Good evening, Ms. Lambert."

"Good evening, Marcus." The elderly chauffeur had been with her father for almost twenty years. He gave her a quick smile. "You look beautiful tonight."

"Thanks," she said, her nerves melting away at the compliment. This was her night. She'd just handled a rather messy PR problem for Tempest's Closet. Her father had even e-mailed her a note that said good job. The only note he'd ever sent her.

She slid into the car as the chauffeur held the door open for her. Her father was on the phone and didn't glance up as the car door closed behind her.

She tried to relax against the plush leather seat of her father's Mercedes-Benz E63 AMG Sedan. The driver sat in the front facing forward, all but invisible to them. She wasn't nervous. Well, maybe a little. It had been so long since she'd allowed herself to want her father's approval. At twenty-eight she was well on her own.

August Lambert, the CEO of Tempest's Closet, was an imposing man. Well over six-feet tall he'd always seemed bigger than life to her when she'd been a little girl. He'd revolutionized the way Americans thought about and purchased clothing with his line of high-end retail Tempest's Closet stores that he had started back in the 1970s and named for her after her birth.

He finished his phone conversation and made a

note in his day-planner before looking over at her. Silence grew between them as he studied her face. She wondered what he saw when he looked at her.

Some people said she looked like her mother but Tempest had never really believed that. Her mother had been one of the most beautiful women Tempest had ever seen. And what she saw reflected back in the mirror was never…beautiful.

"Thank you for meeting with me," he said.

"No problem. What did you want to see me about?"

"I'm promoting Charles Miller."

No small talk or chitchat from him. Just the blunt news that she…well, she hadn't expected.

"Charlie Miller? You've got to be kidding me." Dammit, she'd meant to be calm and cool.

"He's the right man for the job."

She gave her father a hard look—one that she'd picked up from him. "Please tell me you didn't promote him over me because I'm a woman."

"Tempest, I'm not a sexist."

She knew that. She was grasping at straws trying to find a reason. "I'm not so sure, Father. I have more experience than Charlie and am better qualified."

August sighed and rubbed the back of his neck. He stared at the car window watching the Lake Shore Drive scenery pass. She loved Chicago. Sometimes she wished she didn't because then she could simply leave her father and Tempest's Closet far behind.

Her father seemed so unapproachable, so alone. Even though only a few inches of space separated them.

And she felt the distance between them widen. No matter what she tried, she could never get his approval. His respect. A few crazy stunts when she was in her late teens and early twenties and he was going to hold that against her for the rest of her life.

"I haven't done anything to draw attention to myself lately," she said, quietly. This job had become the driving force in her life—no longer a party girl, she'd become a businesswoman. Something she was sure her father would notice.

"There was an article in *Hello!* not a week ago about you and Dean Stratford with pictures of you in your love nest."

"Father, please. You know there's nothing between Dean and me. He's recovering from a serious addiction. He needs support from his friends."

He glanced over at her. "It doesn't matter what I know. The world believes you're a party girl."

She couldn't believe what she was hearing. "The board knows I'm not."

He rubbed a hand over his heart before he put his hands in his lap, linking his fingers together. "I'm more concerned with what the public thinks."

Tempest couldn't argue that point. She almost regretted it but she'd made herself a promise long ago not to apologize for her actions. Though they were most times misconstrued she knew that she always only had the best of intentions where all of her escapades were concerned.

"I think we can overcome that. I've been working with the children's foundation, which is helping my image."

"It's not enough, Tempest. Tempest's Closet is facing some tough times."

"What kind of tough times?" she asked. Being in PR, her focus was more on image than on the company bottom line. But she hadn't heard any rumblings of trouble.

"Nothing you need to worry about."

"I'm an employee, Father. Of course I worry about the stability of the company. Tell me what's going on." She worried more about her father. It had always been one of her biggest fears…losing him. And if anything happened to Tempest's Closet he'd have nothing left to live for.

"It's Renard Investments."

Again? Gavin Renard had been gunning for Tempest's Closet since he'd come onto the investment scene some ten years earlier. He was always trying to man some kind of takeover.

"And Charlie will be a better VP to help you out?" she asked carefully.

"Yes. I need a public relations vice president who can get out there and give us some good spin."

"I think the articles about me should prove I know something about spin," she muttered.

"That's not the kind of spin we want."

"Father, please."

She'd spent her entire life trying to make sure that no one in the world pitied her. Poor little motherless rich girl. Instead she'd made life her party and now she had the feeling she was paying for it. She'd gone to Vassar and gotten her degree. Though she'd heard rumors that her affair with the dean of students was the only reason she'd passed, she knew she'd done the work and Stan had no control over her grades.

She crossed her legs, feeling the smooth silk of her Valentino gown against her skin. She glanced at him out of the corner of her eye.

He sighed and she had her answer. Why she was surprised, she couldn't understand. She hated that she always wanted something from him that he could never deliver.

"I'm sorry, Tempest. My mind is made up."

"Unmake it," she said, starting to lose her temper. Though she desperately wanted to hang on to it. Desperately wanted to find the cool and calm front that her father always presented. Why hadn't she inherited that?

"I think we're done here."

"Not yet. I want you to tell me exactly why I wasn't promoted."

He looked her square in the eye. "You're not responsible enough. I don't trust you to do the job."

The words hurt worse than she'd expected. And she felt the sting of tears in the back of her eyes but refused to cry in front of him. She had, in fact, never cried in front of him. She knew he considered it a cheap feminine ploy used to manipulate men.

"I don't think I'm going to be able to continue to work for you."

"That's your choice, Tempest."

"No, Father, that's yours."

From across the crowded ballroom Gavin Renard caught a glimpse of Tempest Lambert. The socialite was surrounded by a group of people and didn't look the way he'd expected her to. They'd never met, though they attended many of the same functions. To be honest he never really paid that close attention to her until tonight. Maybe it was the way she'd split from August as soon as they'd entered the room.

In her photos she appeared too thin and her mouth was always set in a pout. Her eyes usually held a vacuous expression. As he maneuvered around for a closer look, he noticed that her wide-set blue eyes weren't vacuous tonight. They seethed with something that was either passion or anger.

She wasn't as scary thin as she appeared to be in her photos. He'd thought her an attractive woman when he'd seen her on the cover of *People* magazine but in person she radiated a kind of beauty that left him speechless.

She was his enemy's daughter. So he knew the details of her life. That her mother had died when she was six of complications due to breast cancer. He knew that Tempest had been shipped off to a boarding school in Switzerland and, from all reports, been an excellent student until she turned eighteen and came into the fortune left her by her grandparents.

She'd dropped out of school and joined Europe's party set and never looked back. For six years she partied hard and with little regard for others. There were rumors of affairs with married men, scandalous photos of her in every paper on the continent and occasionally in the U.S.

Then she'd dropped off the party circuit and returned to the States to go to college. The report he'd read of her transcripts had indicated she was an excellent student. But once again she found herself embroiled in a scandal just weeks before graduation when pictures of her and the dean of students surfaced in a local paper.

She glanced up catching him staring. He arched one eyebrow at her, but didn't look away.

"What are you doing?"

Gavin didn't take his gaze from Tempest as he replied to his brother Michael's question.

"Flirting with a pretty lady."

"She's off limits, Gav. Unless you've changed your mind about…?"

"I haven't." He would never change his mind about going after August Lambert's business. August was the reason that Gavin was so successful. The reason he'd driven himself and his employees to take his company to the top. The reason he was here tonight.

Since he'd been old enough to understand the business world, he'd known who August was. At first Gavin had been in awe of what the man accomplished but seeing his methods up close and personal had changed the admiration to disdain.

He'd never forget the excitement he'd felt when he'd heard that August Lambert was opening one of his innovative Tempest's Closet stores in his home town. But he hadn't understood his father's quiet anger toward the man, and had felt a wave of distain for his father and his small-town mind-set in a way only a twelve-year-old boy could.

But in a short while, as the life his father had provided for the Renard family had fallen apart, Gavin had come to understand why his father hated Lambert. Soon Gavin felt hatred for the man, too, slowly turning to a need for revenge that had never left him. The opening of Tempest's Closet had slowly driven all the Main Street shops out of business. Gavin had watched his father struggle to keep the downtown area vital, even going to August Lambert for help. But Lambert had refused.

"Of course you haven't."

"What's your point?"

"Just that you don't want to get involved with someone who works for a company we're going after."

He glanced at Michael. "Since when do I need advice?"

Michael punched him in the arm. "Old man, you always need advice when it comes to your personal life."

"Yeah, right. I think I see Melinda trying to get your attention."

Michael groaned under his breath but turned toward the woman he'd been dating on and off for the last four years. "When are you going to marry her?"

"When you start taking my advice."

"Never?"

"I don't know," Michael said, but the comment felt as if it were directed more at himself than to Gavin.

"Catch you later, Gav. Remember what I said."

"Later, Michael."

As his brother left, Gavin realized that Tempest was no longer talking with the group. The doors opened for seating in the main banquet room. Gavin held back, hoping for one more glance of Tempest.

He felt a hand on his shoulder. Long manicured fingernails rested on the black fabric of his dinner jacket. A sweet sultry scent perfumed the air and he glanced over his shoulder at Tempest.

"Well, hello," he said.

"I saw you watching me."

"Good."

"In some cultures it's considered impolite to stare."

"Your point is?"

She walked around in front of him, staying close

in the crush of people trying to enter the banquet room. "My point is I don't believe we've met."

"Gavin Renard."

"Ah."

"So you've heard of me."

"Vaguely," she said, with a twinkle in her eye. She took another sip of her drink. "I'm Tempest Lambert."

"I know who you are."

"Because of your business interest in Tempest's Closet?" she asked.

Her boldness surprised him. And he wasn't sure why. "Among other things."

She took a sip of the drink in her hand, tipping her head to one side. "Don't believe everything you read about me, Mr. Renard."

She was an enticing bundle of femininity. "I don't."

She reached up and touched his chin. Just her fingertips against the stubble on his face. "That's good because I have a proposition for you."

"I like the sound of that."

"Not that kind of proposition."

"A man can hope."

She turned away, but not before he saw a flash of desire in her eyes.

Interesting.

"What's your offer?" he asked.

"I'm in the market for a job, Gavin," she said.

Just the sound of his name on her lips made everything male in him come to point. He wanted to hear her say his name, but from the tangled sheets of his bed after they'd had wild sex. Not in the middle of this crowded function while he was trying to follow Michael's advice to keep his hands to himself. "No."

She sighed. "I'm very good at PR and I think I can be an asset to your company."

"I can't hire you." He wondered if August had set his daughter up to come to him for a job—maybe with the intent of using her as a corporate spy.

"Don't say no. Not yet. Let me come to your office tomorrow and talk to you. Once you see my resume you might reconsider."

He took her arm. God, her skin was smooth and soft. Softer than a woman's arm should be. He drew her away from the flocks of people and into a quiet part of the hallway. She didn't hesitate to follow him.

He stopped when they were alone and she leaned back against the wall watching him the way a woman watches a man she wants.

"Don't play with me, Tempest."

"I'm not," she said, quietly.

But he knew she was. Gavin hated to think that he might be falling in lust with the daughter of his enemy. Hated that August might have found the one chink in his otherwise impenetrable façade. But then what kind of man would use his daughter like that?

Suspicion and desire warred inside him and he finally gave into desire. He leaned in over her. So close he could see that her blue eyes weren't a pure color but a combination of several different shades.

And that her lashes were thicker than a mink stole. And her lips, ah, hell, her lips were full and wide and as she drew her tongue over the bottom one he remembered exactly how long it had been since he'd held a woman in his arms.

And he couldn't trust her. His best bet would be to scare her off with a bold pass. From what he'd read of her, she was used to pampered boys who lived off their family's fortunes.

"Gavin?"

"I don't need you in my PR department... but..." he said.

"Don't say it," she warned him.

He didn't voice his request, just tugged her a little closer and brought his mouth to her ear. She shivered as his breath brushed over her and he felt an answering spread of sensation. He felt the first tingling of arousal in his loins.

"It's obvious we're attracted to each other," he whispered.

She pulled back from him. "I am attracted to you, which makes no sense at all."

Hell, he knew that. But he wanted her. More than he should. This wasn't logical or rational but she felt so right.

Too right. It reminded him that the deep freeze he'd carefully existed in while focusing on his plan of revenge was starting to thaw. In her gaze he saw a hint of sadness and the kind of determination that played havoc with his control.

She closed her eyes. He saw her skin flush at his words and her shoulders sank back, lifting her breasts toward him.

He caressed the long line of her cheekbones. Her skin was softer than the sea mist. Her lashes drifted down as he explored the angles and curves of her face. He traced the lines of her lips as they parted under his touch. He stroked his thumb over her full lower lip, watched the natural pink color of her lips darken.

She tipped her head back and leaned the slightest bit toward him. There was a bit of haughtiness in her that intrigued him. He wanted to take her in his arms and see how haughty she looked after he ravished her mouth with his kisses.

She shrugged her shoulder. "I'm not looking for an affair, Gavin. I'm looking for a job."

He knew he'd never hire her but he didn't want to just let her walk away from him. And he knew that was her intent. "I can see you tomorrow at eleven."

"Great. Prepare to be amazed," she said, walking away.

TWO

Tempest had dressed for her interview with Gavin Renard with care. Her black Chanel suit was a classic and she wore it like a security blanket. She loved the feeling of the lined summer-weight wool skirt against her legs. She paired it with a pair of ultra-thin sheer French hose and some Ferragamos that were understated and sophisticated.

But still she was nervous. Her hands trembled as she took a sip of the coffee Gavin's secretary Marilyn had gotten for her. She hated being that betrayed by her own emotions and forced herself to rehearse in her head what she planned to say one more time.

She wasn't only thinking of a new job. She was

thinking of Gavin Renard the man, and that ticked her off. It was one thing to think of him as a way to make her father sit up and take notice of the kind of executive he let slip through his fingers. But who would have thought that this man could mess with her plans? Of course, to be honest, she hadn't had much of a plan when she walked over to him. She'd just wanted to meet the man her father was so obsessed with and get a bead on whether or not there was something there she could use to make her father reconsider her for the promotion. Those plans had gone out the window when she'd realized how attracted she was to Gavin.

"Ms. Lambert?"

"Yes?"

"Mr. Renard will see you now."

She smiled her thanks at the secretary and put her coffee cup on the end-table. She took a deep breath before getting to her feet. Her mother had always said to take her time. That it was better to arrive late and prepared for an event than on time and unrehearsed.

In her mind she cranked up "Welcome to the Jungle" by Guns 'N' Roses. Then she picked up her briefcase and walked into his office.

Gavin stood when she entered. His shirt was a deep blue that made his gray eyes seem even more brilliant in the office lighting. He was taller than she remembered and she realized her heels the other evening had given her an extra inch of height that these didn't. She smiled up at him as the soundtrack in her head changed from energizing rock to Sade's "Smooth Operator."

He smelled really good, too. The spicy male scent enveloped her as he held out his hand. The slow sensuous music in her head made the office background drop away.

"Good morning, Tempest."

She shook her head. His big hand totally engulfed hers. She held on longer than she should have before pulling back and nervously clearing her throat. No, she thought. She wasn't nervous. She was calm, cool, totally collected and together.

"Good morning, Gavin. Did you enjoy the benefit last night?"

"Yes. Please have a seat."

So much for small talk. It was clear to her that Gavin wasn't interested in the social niceties that she'd built her life around. She made a mental note to remember that. She sat down and pulled her resume from her briefcase.

"Thank you for agreeing to this meeting."

"I'm still not sure why I did," he said.

For a minute she thought this was a big mistake and then their eyes met and she realized he'd agreed for the same reason she'd asked. *Mutual attraction.* She knew this was an impossible situation. He'd never be able to forget she was her father's daughter.

But she wasn't one who backed down. She'd

made it her life's goal to always keep moving forward. Never looking back. She wanted Gavin to see her as a prospective employee first and a woman second. And to totally forget she was a Lambert. Today that seemed really important. She was just another out-of-work businessperson.

"Because you're a shrewd businessman who knows a good thing when he sees it," she said, handing him her resume. Stay cool and confident, she reminded herself.

"I definitely liked what I saw the other night."

She smiled at him. This might be easier than she'd expected. She could play on the attraction flowing between them like a high-voltage current.

"Me, too."

He gave her a half-smile. It was an arrogant expression from a man who was confident of his appeal to the opposite sex. But then she wasn't lacking in confidence herself. She crossed her legs letting the hem of her skirt ride up the slightest bit. His eyes tracked the movement.

"What exactly is it that you do, Tempest?"

"I'm in PR. I've been responsible for most of the press you've seen about Tempest's Closet for the last three years."

"What makes you think I've been watching your press?"

"Please, Gavin. I think we both know that you are aware of every move that Tempest's Closet makes."

He shrugged one shoulder and leaned back in his chair. "I am."

He said nothing else, letting the silence build between them. She couldn't stand it because she knew he was building the case against her in his head. Finding the words to tell her to take her briefcase and walk out his door.

And this was her only option. Her only chance to really make sure her father realized that he'd let her slip through his fingers…for good this time.

"Just look at my resume. I think you'll see I'm more than you expected."

"You already are," he said.

She was a little startled by that. She handed him her resume and sank back into the chair.

Her resume was more impressive than he'd expected it to be. He didn't know why he was surprised. He'd made a few phone calls this morning and found out more information on his enemy's daughter than she'd probably be comfortable with him having.

Everyone he spoke to mentioned her keen intelligence and her ability to put people at ease. She had a knack for finding the morsel of good news in the worst situation and spinning it out until the media was running with the idea she fed them.

In short she'd be the perfect addition to his team if she weren't August Lambert's daughter. But she was. And nothing could change that.

He hadn't been able to get anything from his Tempest's Closet source on why Tempest was job hunting. But he'd figure that out today. See if there was anything in her leaving Tempest's Closet that he could use to his advantage.

She shifted her legs again and he tracked the movement with his eyes. She had dynamite legs. All he could think of was how smooth they'd feel to his touch. The few glimpses he'd had of her thigh were enough to make his fingertips tingle.

He frowned and forced himself to study her resume. He wasn't getting involved with her. He wasn't doing the lust thing with this woman. It had nothing to do with the advice of his brother and everything to do with focus. He couldn't afford any kind of distraction now that he was so close to his goal. Ten years of walking the path of revenge and he wasn't going to lose it this close to the finish line.

"Why did you leave Tempest's Closet?" he asked. No one knew the answer to that.

"I had a differing opinion with my boss."

"You mean your father, right?"

She sat up straighter in the chair and put both of her feet on the floor. Staring him straight in the eye. "I didn't get the job because of nepotism. I worked hard to prove myself within our charitable foundation before making the move to Tempest's Closet."

"Of course you did." He knew she'd gotten the job the same way every other employee had. Through her qualifications and skills. In fact, she'd probably had to work harder.

He knew how contentious her relationship was with August. He also didn't want her to leave his office until he figured out if there was a way that he could exploit that. There had to be something here he was missing.

"I'm not going to argue the point. If you can't see what an advantage I'd be to your organization then you're not the man I thought you were."

He glanced up at her then and realized he felt a grudging respect for her. She fought dirty…well she fought to win. And he always respected winning except when August Lambert won.

And somehow this daughter of his had to be the key to bringing him down. No, she was the key to twisting the pain of losing when August fell. And the old man was going down.

Right now, though, he needed some answer from her. He should be treating this like an interview. Keeping his eyes off her legs and focusing on what she was doing here. "Why did you go into PR?"

She relaxed in her seat, crossing those long legs again. "It seemed like the right fit for me. I know a lot of people in the media."

"Is it only because of your contacts?" he asked. There had to be more. She'd been hounded by the press for years before she'd started working in PR. He thought it was a very shrewd move on her behalf to turn that around. To make dealing with the press her career.

She swallowed hard. "I just wanted to give them something real to print. To move the focus off of me and onto something else. That's why I started with the charity. I knew no one would take me seriously until I changed my reputation in the media."

He respected what she'd done. To some extent he'd made a similar decision when he'd entered the investing world. His family had started with nothing and he'd turned that around. Taking the very thing that had ruined his father and making it his own strength.

"Good move."

"Thanks," she said, flashing him a grin that stopped him in his tracks. She had a wonderful smile.

"Okay, as impressive as your qualifications are, I can't hire you."

Her smile disappeared and she blinked a few times. "Is it because I'm a Lambert?"

Yes, he thought. She had to see he couldn't hire her. But he didn't want her to just walk out his door. He wanted to see her again. "Only partly. I don't have any openings in my PR department."

"But you said partly. Don't think about who my father is."

"It's a big part of who you are, Tempest. Even if I had an opening, I wouldn't hire you."

"You're missing out on one hell of a PR exec, Gavin," she said, standing up and gathering her briefcase.

He stood as well and walked over to the door, blocking her from leaving.

"I think if I hired you, I'd miss out on a hell of a woman, Tempest."

Her eyes widened and he knew she was debating the next move to make. He wondered then if he wasn't the only one fishing for information. If he wasn't the only one who was dealing with emotions he didn't understand exactly.

That's what he wanted to find out. He'd never be able to trust her in his office but in his bed…that was something all together different.

"Are you saying you want to date me?"

He thought about that for a long minute. Dating her really wasn't any different than hiring her. She was still his enemy's daughter…but he'd been focused on revenge for too long.

Barely an inch of space was between their bodies. He smelled even better up close than he had when she'd shaken his hand. He crowded closer to her and she fought not to back up. But in the end her need for personal space won out and she inched away from him.

He was all arrogant male. Totally sure of himself and his impact on her. And she wished she could prove him wrong. Wished she could take a step away from him and dismiss him with a snooty comment that would put him in his place. Remind him that she was the daughter of August Lambert.

"You're crowding me," she said carefully. She was completely out of her element with this man.

She didn't know him well enough to know the best way to deal with him. She only knew one thing for certain. She wasn't leaving this office without some kind of offer. Her pride was on the line, and to be honest, pride was the only thing she'd ever really had that was her own.

"Good."

"Why good?"

"I like it when you get your back up."

"I don't *get my back up*. I'm a well-bred young lady." No one had ever said anything like that to her before. He treated her like he wasn't impressed by her pedigree, which of course he wasn't. He disliked her father. Did that feeling transfer to her, as well?

"I'm not a well-bred man," he said.

She realized she knew practically nothing about Gavin. There was something in his tone that warned her that he hadn't had the same privileged upbringing she had. "Well, for future reference, I get haughty."

"I'll make a note."

She couldn't believe their meeting had come to this. Flirting. She was flirting with a man who had pretty much said he wasn't going to do what she wanted him to. And for some reason that didn't hurt as much as she'd thought it might. But then she was a master at hiding the hurt inflicted on her by the men in her life. And Gavin technically wasn't in her life.

Gavin was a long shot for a job from the beginning. But she wasn't ready to throw in the towel yet.

"I've got a deal for you," she said.

"I'm not interested in making deals."

"You're kidding. Your entire career is based on making deals."

He leaned closer to her, bracing his arms on the wall on either side of her head. Just like that she was trapped. He brought the heel of his hand down on her shoulder and tangled his fingers in her hair.

"Is it a business proposition?" he asked, using his grip on her hair to tip her head to the side. His thumb traced the line of her jaw.

He touched her so carefully. Like she was something fragile and breakable. It wasn't the way people usually treated her. Everyone knew she was tough as nails. Ballsy and brash and haughty. No vulnerabilities.

"Tempest?"

What the heck was he talking about? Then she remembered. She wanted to make a deal with him. She wanted to convince him to hire her. And she'd use whatever she had to get his attention. If that meant playing up the attraction between them then so be it.

"Kind of."

"Kind of?"

She thought quickly, trying to blunt the impact of his body next to hers. She closed her eyes so that she wouldn't have to look into his brilliant gaze. But that just made her more aware of his body heat and the yummy scent of his aftershave.

She cleared her throat. "You give me one media event to handle and if I do a good job you hire me."

He looked her straight in the eyes and she saw his answer before he said anything. She put her finger over his lips. Traced the lower one when his lips parted.

"Tempest…"

"Don't say no."

He leaned down so that when he spoke his breath brushed her ear. She shivered in awareness and had the feeling that Gavin knew exactly what he was about when it came to seducing women. And it had been so long since she'd been with a man. Three years to be exact. Three long years while she'd focused on her career. And look where that had gotten her.

"Tempest…"

"What?" she asked, cocking her head to the side so that her mouth was angled right next to his—a breath away. She wet her lips and watched his eyes following the movement of her tongue.

"I can't hire the daughter of my enemy."

She was afraid he'd say that. She had known this was a long shot, but she'd spent her entire life battling against a man who was resolved to feel nothing for her. She didn't give up easily and she wasn't going to now either.

"I'm not your enemy," she said. "This could work to your advantage."

He shook his head.

"Gavin, this is my last chance to prove to him that he's made a mistake. I'm not leaving your office unless you change your mind."

"An ultimatum?"

"A promise. I'm not the flighty-flirty heiress you've read about in the papers. I'm a well-educated asset that could be working for you."

He sighed and moved back from her. "I'm not making any promises, but I'll consider you if there is an opening."

"That's all I ask."

"Until then…"

"Yes?"

"Dinner?"

"What about it?" she asked. She wasn't going to accept an invitation like that. She was, after all, Tempest Lambert.

"Would you have dinner with me tonight?"

"I'm busy."

"Liar."

"I do have plans. You can join me if you want. I'll pick you up here at seven."

Three

Gavin had been surprised when he'd gotten the e-mail from Tempest asking him to meet her at the Gillock Gallery on north Ravenswood Avenue. He'd worked later than he'd planned to and then made his way across town to the gallery opening for an artist that Gavin had never heard of before, Pablo Montovan.

He mentioned Tempest's name at the door and was told to go right in. He got a glass of wine from the waiter and walked through the room stopping to study the art. He'd never taken time for the niceties in life. Michael collected sculptures and their mother had an affinity for photography. But Gavin wasn't interested in anything unless it brought him closer to his goal of bringing down August.

For the first time he realized how one-dimensional his life was. How work-centric he was. He took a sip of the California chardonnay and studied the portraiture. It depicted a crowd of people in the center of the canvas on a solid block of color. As he stood there he realized how alone each person was. Isolated in a sea of many.

He glanced back and came face-to-face with Tempest.

A soft feminine hand rested on his shoulder. "Like it?"

"I'm not sure."

"Why not?" she asked. She wore a simple cocktail dress in black and white. But the dress was anything but simple on her.

He shrugged, not planning on answering that.

"This piece—Waiting #7. Makes me feel kind of sad. Not a good feeling of expectation. But like they are all waiting for something they don't want."

He took another sip of his wine.

"Come on, Gavin, tell me what you see."

"I'm not really into art," he said, afraid any comments he made would reveal too much of his own inner turmoil.

He saw the disappointment in her eyes and told himself it didn't matter. He'd only come tonight out of curiosity. Not about the art but about the woman he couldn't figure out.

"Nice turn out," he said.

She sighed and then smiled at him. But it wasn't her usual brilliant expression.

"Yes, it is. I was worried that Pablo wouldn't get the crowds he does in Europe."

"You're a friend of the artist?" he asked. There seemed to be few circles where she didn't know someone. He knew that would be a great asset in a PR director. For a minute he wondered if she had been legit in his office. Was she really just looking for a job? Or was he right to suspect that her father might be using her as a pawn?

"Yes. I want you to meet him. I noticed that the lobby of your building is a little bare. Pablo does some stunning murals."

Gavin followed her through the crowd, stopping when she did and engaging in small talk with people he had nothing in common with. Yet slowly he realized he didn't mind it. He liked listening to Tempest and the way she talked to others.

She effortlessly put everyone at ease. Finding obscure connections between the various groups and starting conversations that weren't frivolous. She introduced him as simply the head of an investment firm and when he noticed a few raised eyebrows from people who'd obviously heard of the feud between him and August, she simply smiled it off.

Was that her intent? To plant the seeds of doubt in public so that his investors would get jittery and pull back?

He pulled her to the side of the crowded room.

The noise of conversation and music filled the air but he found a quiet hallway tucked out of the way.

"What?" she asked.

"Why did you invite me here tonight?"

She lifted one shoulder and glanced back at the crowd. She was ill at ease for the first time since he'd met her, her normal boldness stifled by this quiet hallway and his questions.

"I wanted a chance to get to know you better," she said at last. "I'm not going to lie to you. I'm still hoping to convince you to give me a job."

"Why do you want to get to know me better?" he asked, completely ignoring the job thing. He'd already made up his mind not to hire her, nothing would change it. "Are you spying on me for your father?"

She wrapped her arm around her waist and took two steps away from him. There was such hurt in her eyes that he wanted to apologize but he didn't. He'd made a plausible assumption.

"I'm not like that, Gavin."

She waited and he sensed that she wanted him to say something that would make things right between them. But he didn't have the words.

She turned away but he stopped her with his hand on her elbow, tugging her to a stop. "Don't be offended. It was a logical theory."

"And you're always logical, aren't you?"

"Yes. I don't understand you." He'd learned from watching his father that emotion had no place in the decision-making process.

"What's to understand? I want a chance to work for you and I'm attracted to you. I thought we agreed to at least explore the attraction."

Did they? He wasn't sure now what he'd agreed to. Her skin was ultra soft and he ran his finger over the flesh of her inner arm. He knew he should stop, that the touch was too intimate for a public place, but she felt so good. No one should have skin that soft.

Goose flesh spread down her arm and she turned to face him. "You can't argue the attraction."

"I don't want to," he admitted. Though it wasn't logical, it made no sense to confess to feelings that he knew weren't sensible.

"But you don't exactly want to embrace it, either," she said.

"True."

She turned away from him and this time he let her slip free. He'd seen the hurt in her eyes. What had it been like growing up with August as a father?

Tempest was the first to admit she didn't always handle herself well with men she wanted to impress. But normally she was able to insulate herself enough from them that she didn't allow any of their comments to hurt her.

Gavin was different. She really wanted to make a good impression on him. Yet everything she did he saw as a move in the ongoing business of one-upmanship he had with her father.

"Let me introduce you to Pablo and then we can say our goodbyes," she said. She had the feeling no matter what she did to show him she was qualified to work for him, he wasn't going to change his mind.

"I don't want to meet Pablo."

"I promise you won't regret it."

He wrapped his hand around her neck and drew her back against his body. Lowering his head he inhaled deeply and she held herself still in his embrace, afraid to move.

"I regret everything about this night."

There was a finality to his words that she wished she didn't understand but it was too late. He was saying goodbye. She swallowed and stepped away from him, felt his fingers in her hair until she moved far enough away that the strands fell to her shoulders again.

There were a million thoughts rushing around her head. Regret of her own that she'd never get to know this man she was attracted to. Some anger at her father because if not for him...well, if not for him she wouldn't have approached Gavin so she knew that anger wasn't justified. It was just...oh, man, she wanted him. Him, not any other man, and it had been a long time since that had happened.

How had that happened? She was careful not to let anyone too close to her.

"Tempest?"

She shook her head, realizing she'd been standing there staring at him. "You really need something to soften the austerity of the lobby. Art puts people at ease." She needed to keep talking about his business. To somehow keep that knowledge in the front of her mind. If she stopped and let herself think about the fact that she'd been rejected again, she might break down.

"Okay," he said quietly.

She led him out of the hallway and back into the main gallery room. A buffet table was set against the windows that looked out on the street. There was a small jazz combo in the corner and a postage stamp-sized dance floor.

She moved into the crowd away from him. Trying to not be hyper aware of where he was but it was impossible. As she moved through the room she realized the truth of her life.

People smiled at her, air-kissed her cheek. Complimented her haute-couture outfit and made references to events they had attended together in the past. And the truth of the evening kept circling in her head. She kept hearing that voice that she hated listening to, the one that never let her flinch from the truth. The one that made her want to cry.

The truth was that she had a life filled with things just as her father did. A life filled with acquaintances instead of friends. A life empty of any real joy or real emotions.

And for one moment she'd come close to finding someone who'd maybe fill that emptiness.

She finished her Bellini in one long swallow and deposited the glass on the tray of a passing waiter.

Good God, she was getting depressing. She needed to get out of Chicago for a while.

Chicago was the place where her greatest hurts were. It was the city she'd been living in when her mother had died. And now she had this new one.

"Got a minute, Tempest?"

"Sure," she said, surprised to see Charlie Miller at this event. Though he was a crackerjack PR man, he didn't move in the same circles she did.

"Um, first I want to say, I'm sorry you didn't get the promotion."

She genuinely liked Charlie and with a few more years experience he was going to be exactly what her father needed. He was smart and savvy but a little young and inexperienced.

"As my father said, 'the best man got the job,'" she said.

He flushed. "I hope I can live up to that expectation."

"Of course you will. So what did you want?"

"I was hoping you'd have some time in your schedule to sit down and talk about some of the projects that were pending when you left. Kind of get me up to speed."

She had left abruptly. Like a spoiled child when she'd realized she'd once again let her father disappoint her. "Yes, I can. But I can't come by the office. How about Starbucks on Michigan tomorrow?"

"Fine. Ten would be good for me."

The small talk continued for a few more minutes before Kali interrupted them. Grateful for the rescue,

Tempest smiled at her friend. Kali Trevaine was one of Tempest's oldest friends. Kali's mom, Talia, had been a supermodel, one of the first that Tempest's Closet had used in their American marketing campaigns. In those early days her mother had been very active in the company and had brought Tempest to all the photo shoots.

She and Kali had bonded young. Playing in the clothes and getting into mischief. When Tempest had been a teenager and her father had wanted her to stay at school for the summers, Talia and Kali had invited her into their home. Kali was the closest thing Tempest had to a sister.

"What was that about?"

"He's the guy my father replaced me with."

"Ah, the competition. I think you could have taken him in a physical match."

Tempest laughed as she knew Kali wanted her to. It was true that Charlie was a small man, only five-seven and slim. She probably could take him if she were given to doing such a thing.

"Is that your new reality TV show idea? A corporate version of *Celebrity Death Match?*"

"Ah, no, I hadn't thought beyond you. But that thought has merit."

"Please, I was kidding. I don't want to see something like that on TV."

"Maybe America does," Kali said.

"Excuse me, ladies."

Tempest was surprised Gavin had sought her out

again. But maybe he wanted to meet Kali. At five-nine she was thin and stunningly beautiful. Her coffee-colored skin and exotically shaped eyes drew men to her like bees to honey. But Tempest was also disappointed that she'd been so strongly attracted to a man who could go so quickly from wanting her to wanting her friend.

"Yes, Gavin?"

"Dance with me," he said.

He nodded to Kali as he drew Tempest through the crowd to the dance floor.

"I thought we'd said goodbye," she said, as he drew her into his arms.

"Not yet."

She rested her head on his shoulder as the band played a slow jazzy number. She knew this wasn't real and wouldn't last, but for this instant she felt at home in his arms.

There was no way in hell that this woman belonged with him.

She could never be more than a means to an end. But it didn't feel that way and for just one moment he shut down the logical part of his mind and just held her.

The music swirled around them as did the other couples on the small dance floor, but when Tempest lowered her head to his shoulder the rest of the world disappeared.

He knew this was an emotional reaction. Tried to

justify the feelings with the knowledge that anything he started wouldn't go any further than this dance floor.

And that made the need sharpen inside him. He wanted her. His skin felt too tight and his blood flowed heavier in his veins. He'd been jealous when he'd seen her talking with that skinny man earlier. And he didn't like that.

He wasn't a jealous man—he just never permitted himself to connect to any of the women he'd dated. He reserved those emotions solely for his mother and his brother.

But with Tempest everything was different, dammit. He didn't like it. He wasn't a possessive man but each time Tempest had stopped with a group to chat he'd found himself resentful that he wasn't in the group.

"Did you talk to Pablo?"

"Yes," he said, not interested in discussing another man with her. This covetousness was unfounded. She wasn't his. He shouldn't feel so possessive but he did.

"Did you ask him to do a mural—"

"No, Tempest. I don't want to talk about art tonight."

"Then why did you come to a showing?" she asked. There was something in her voice that stopped his impatient answer. That hint of vulnerability he'd noticed before. It roused more than his possessiveness—it made him want to protect her. To ensure that she wasn't hurt.

"Because *you* asked me to," he said, quietly.

She rubbed her cheek against his shoulder and he

wished they were both naked so he could feel the softness of her skin against his own.

"I think there is more to it than that," she said.

Of course there was more to it. Nothing with Tempest was easy. It was complicated by matters that had been a part of his life for too long now. He almost wished they'd delayed their first date until after the November board meeting of Tempest's Closet. After he'd dismantled her father's empire and finally had the revenge he'd spent years working toward.

He knew that she'd never have anything to do with him once he took over her father's company. Sure, the relationship with her father was strained, but August was all that Tempest had. Though a boy at the time, Gavin could remember the stories of Tempest Lambert...poor little rich girl. The Lambert family had one of those curses that the media liked to play up. And Gavin had learned one thing from all the articles he'd read about her. She was an incredibly loyal woman.

Her loyalty to Lambert was obvious to Gavin even thought she'd come to Renard Investments for a job. She was still a Lambert and still passionate about Tempest's Closet.

He wondered what that felt like. He wondered if August had any idea how lucky he was to have someone so loyal to him that no matter how cruelly he treated her, she'd still be there. And for just a moment he wanted to shake Tempest for always allowing her father to hurt her.

"We already discussed this."

"Yes, we did and I thought we'd found closure but somehow I'm back in your arms again."

His gut clenched at her words. He wanted her in his arms. Really in his bed. Naked and willing under him. Only then would he be able to find any closure to the relentless need that kept hammering through his body.

He tightened his grip on her back, slowly sliding his hands to her hips. His fingers flexing and sinking into her soft curves. He drew her nearer to him until her breasts rested against his chest.

Her breath caught in her throat and she tipped her head back, looking up at him with those wide blue eyes of hers. He saw the answering need in her gaze. Saw that she wanted him with the same insane passion. Saw that this wasn't going to be easy for her to walk away from either.

And strangely that was just what he needed to justify lowering his head to hers right there on the crowded dance floor. He forgot that public displays of affection were taboo for him because they made the public and the stockholders doubt his ability to run his business. He forgot that she was the daughter of his rival. He forgot everything except the fact that he hadn't tasted her lips and he wanted to.

Needed to. He wasn't going to last another second until he knew if her kiss was as flat-out hot as he expected it to be.

He lifted one hand from her hips, tangled his fingers in her softer-than-sable hair and tilted her head back.

She gasped as he lowered his mouth over hers and he wasn't tentative in taking her. He thrust his tongue deep into her mouth. He gave her no chance to respond, just wielded his will over her.

She tasted of the slightly sweet drink she'd had earlier and raspberry lip gloss. She wrapped both her hands around his shoulders and shifted in his embrace, her tongue sliding against his. Her hands tangling in the hair at the back of his neck.

Blood roared in his ears as he rubbed his hand up and down her back. He felt the fragility of her spine, the fineness of her slim body. He lifted his head and rubbed his lips along the line of her jaw and down to her neck.

She tasted again of that essence of woman that he was coming to associate only with her. She moaned deep in her throat as he thrust his tongue into her mouth. Her tongue stroked tentatively against his.

Sliding his hands down her back he cupped her hips and pulled her more firmly against his body. He'd meant to keep the embrace light because they were in the middle of the dance floor.

He rubbed his growing erection against her and she made a soft sound in the back of her throat. Her nails dug into his shoulders through the layer of his shirt. She undulated against him.

He lifted his head. Her eyes were closed and face was flushed with desire. He knew that it would take very little for him to persuade her to have sex with him tonight. And part of him wanted to do that, to take what he needed.

His heart beat too quickly in his chest and the lust that had taken entire control of his body abated at the fear that was slowly creeping through him. He wanted her more than he should.

He had to stop this insanity and leave. He rubbed his finger over her wet lips and took a step back.

"Goodbye," he said, knowing that he was going to have a hell of a time forgetting her.

She lifted her hand toward him and he was tempted to stay. Tempted to say the hell with the inappropriateness of their relationship and take something he wanted even though it didn't fit into his plans.

A camera flash went off to his left. He caught a glimpse of a man running through the crowd. This is what a relationship with Tempest would be like, he thought.

"Gavin?"

He shook his head and walked away without looking back. And it was one of the hardest thing he'd ever done.

Four

Tempest was tired, cranky and out of sorts when she left her condo the next morning for her meeting with Charlie. And she wasn't very well prepared. She hadn't gone back to the office after she'd decided to quit working for her father, so she had no notes other than the things she'd kept in her head.

And this might not be the best morning for a meeting because all she could think about was Gavin. She hated the fact that they'd both agreed to part ways. She knew it was the most sensible thing to do but she ached for him.

That kiss last night had made it impossible for her to do anything other than moon over the man. And that ticked her off. The only man who'd had the power to completely make her crazy before had been her father. Of course that was an entirely different thing.

All conversations stopped when she entered the Starbucks on Michigan Avenue. She tried to pretend that she hadn't noticed. But she felt like a huge spotlight was on her. She glanced around the barista trying to find something else to engage her attention when she saw a discarded newspaper. She snagged it from the table while she waited to order her coffee.

She skimmed the headlines and then flipped to the society page, hoping her presence at Pablo's opening got him some additional press. Her jaw dropped as she saw the picture of her and Gavin. She hadn't even noticed the flashbulb when he'd been kissing her.

But there they were in the middle of the dance floor. Totally wrapped up in each other. She touched her own lips as they started to tingle. There'd been so much passion in that kiss. She could still feel his body pressed against her. She glanced at the caption and felt the blood drain from her face.

Sleeping with the enemy? Tempest Lambert never shies away from scandal but cavorting with Gavin Renard the CEO of Tempest's Closet's fiercest competition is a little over the top even by her standards.

She fumbled in her purse for her sunglasses and donned them quickly. It was too late to really disguise herself but the glasses provided a shield that no matter how false, she needed.

She dug around her bag until she found her cell

phone and dialed Kali's number. She didn't know what to do and needed her friend.

A call beeped in before Kali answered and she glanced down at the caller ID wondering if it would be her dad. It wasn't. The number was one she couldn't identify. She let it go to the voicemail and switched back to Kali's line.

"Hello?" she asked when she heard silence on the open line.

"Tempest?"

Thank God, Kali was home. "Yes, did you see the paper?"

"No. What's up?"

The man in front of her glanced over his shoulder at her and she realized this was not a conversation she wanted to have standing in line at Starbucks. She walked out of the coffee shop and down the sidewalk to a quiet area.

"There's a picture of Gavin and I."

"From last night?"

"Uh…yes."

"From the dance floor?" Kali asked again and the speculation in her friend's voice made her want to cringe.

She'd openly courted the press for years after she'd graduated from finishing school. Used them as a way to make her father notice her even though he'd always made it a point to ignore her. And she'd regretted it for the last few years but it was, of course, too late to go back and change things. But this picture she resented the most.

"Yes," she said to Kali. "What am I going to do? Gavin didn't want to date me for precisely this reason."

"He wasn't exactly an unwilling participant."

"Kali!"

"Well, that's the truth."

"I know. I was just hoping…" she stopped before she said any more. She'd been hoping that Gavin would have a change of heart, but now she doubted he would.

"Oh, honey. I was hoping, too, that this guy would be different."

Sometimes she wished Kali didn't know her as well as she did. But right now it was nice to know she wasn't alone. That she had someone in her corner. "There's no way the tabloids aren't going to pick this up."

"You're right. So what's the plan?"

"I don't know. I have to think this through."

"I don't like the sound of that," Kali said.

"Maybe there's a way to make this a win-win."

"For who? You?"

"Me and Gavin."

"Be careful."

"I will be." She hung up the phone and waked slowly back to her car. Her mind was moving swiftly over the possibilities. There had to be a way for this to work to their advantage.

With the press playing up the fact that they were

involved, she might be able to convince Gavin to make their relationship real. She made a quick call to Charlie to cancel their appointment.

She didn't have Gavin's number but knew where his office was so she drove there. She parked and walked into the building wondering what she was going to say to him. But it was nerves ruling her now. It was excitement and the thought that she'd found a way to spend more time with him.

She still wanted a job. A job for her father's rival would anger her father but it was more than that. She wanted the job to prove that someone else had thought her worthy.

She stopped for a minute near the bank of elevators. Nerves simmered again as she realized that Gavin might have had the same thought that the newspaper did. That sleeping with his enemy's daughter would be a nice twist. And she had some doubts for the first time since she'd decided to come to his building.

Then again she'd planned to use him to make her father angry. Could she really begrudge him the same thing?

Tempest heard someone come up behind her near the bank of elevators. Her gut instinct was to try to make herself smaller so she wouldn't be recognized, but instead she put her shoulders back and stood taller

"Tempest?"

Gavin. "Hi. Have you seen the newspaper?"

He nodded. "Let's talk in my office."

* * *

Gavin focused on the fact that he'd correctly predicted that Tempest would come to his office when she saw the photo instead of on the fact that they were alone in the elevator and he wanted to hit the emergency stop button and pull her into his arms.

Only the knowledge that Michael was waiting in his office stayed his hand. He had a vague idea that seducing Tempest wasn't off limits now. Everyone was going to believe they were involved anyway. But the way he felt about her was too intense. Could his logical side stay focused on business if he was involved in an affair with her?

His libido said who the hell cared. But he knew better than to let his groin make a decision.

"Why are you staring at me?" she asked.

There was none of the ballsy attitude she'd had the first time she'd visited his office. "Probably because you're wearing your sunglasses inside."

She flushed a little and shifted her brown Coach bag from her right shoulder to her left. "Oh, I'd forgotten them."

He leaned against the walnut paneling in the elevator and tried to look like he was at ease.

"Why do you have them on?" It was an overcast morning, no sun in sight.

She straightened the large dark glasses on her face and then glanced up at him. "I was in Starbucks when I saw the paper."

"I don't understand."

"Of course, you wouldn't."

He just waited and she sighed and wrapped an arm around her waist. "People stare at me when I'm out. And after I saw that picture of us in the paper I felt…well, I just put the glasses on because it gives me the illusion of hiding."

In that instant he knew whatever else happened between them he wasn't going to be able to just let her walk back out of his door. He wanted to pull her into his arms and hold her tight to his side. But dammit, he wasn't a protector. He was a destroyer. He knew that. Even his success in business had come from buying up failing companies and taking them apart.

He took her sunglasses off and folded them in his hand. She stared up at him and he saw the truth in her gaze. The vulnerability that she never let the world see.

He cupped her face in his palm and tipped her head up so that she could see the truth in his eyes.

"You don't need to hide from me."

She chewed on her lower lip. He lowered his head and brushed her mouth with his. He wanted to deepen the contact but restraint was needed now. Later when they were alone in his office…

"I think I need to hide most of all from you."

"Why?"

"Because you see me in ways that no one else does."

The elevator doors opened before he could respond and his brother stood there in the hallway waiting for them.

"We'll finish this discussion later."

"Will we?" she asked in that sassy way of hers. She was getting herself back from the shock of seeing that photo. He was glad for it. He could deal with the ballsy woman better than the vulnerable one.

"I just said we would."

"Well then I guess your word is law."

"Yes, it is," Michael said.

Gavin gave his brother a hard look but Michael just grinned at him. "Trust me. You can't win when you go up against Gavin."

"I'm not so sure that's true," Tempest said.

"I don't believe we've met. I'm Michael Renard."

"Tempest Lambert."

She shook hands with Michael and made small talk as they walked down the hallway to the executive offices. Gavin envied his brother many things but in this moment he wished he had the ability to loosen up the way Michael did. Then again, Michael lacked the focus and intensity that were so much a part of his own make up.

As they entered his office, Gavin told his secretary they weren't to be disturbed. Tempest and Michael fell silent as they took a seat in the guest chairs.

Gavin walked over to the windows that looked out over Lake Michigan. He'd spent the morning going over different courses of action, trying to find the one that would best suit this situation. The one he could use to his advantage.

For once he didn't trust his own logic. Didn't trust the plan he'd settled on. All because of the one variable he couldn't control—Tempest.

Tempest cleared her throat and he turned around to face her.

"I'm sorry," she said. "You shouldn't have to pay the price just because my life is one big goldfish bowl."

"You don't have to apologize. I'm the one who kissed you."

She flushed and glanced at his brother.

"Um…I'll leave you two to discuss this. Let me know when you need me."

Michael left the office closing the door behind him. Tempest stood up.

"I'm not sure where we go from here, Gavin. Short of me finding another man to go out with— that might draw the press away from you, but I'm not interested in anyone else."

She wasn't going to date anyone else if he had anything to say about it. "That's not necessary. I think the best thing to do would be for us to have an affair. See where this attraction leads."

Gavin stared at her for a moment and realized that the only plan he wanted to enact was one where they were together. There was the added bonus that the press from any type of relationship they had would drive her father crazy.

He wasn't the kind to talk about business outside of the office so even if she were some kind of corporate spy—which he doubted—there was no information she could take back to her father from him.

He didn't allow himself to think of Tempest except in terms of an affair. He hoped like hell that the attraction he felt for her was only a sexual thing and once it ran its course they could both move on.

An affair. She wanted one with him but he was so cold when he suggested it. She hesitated. Was she really going to start a relationship with a man who could be so aloof?

"That sounds so romantic," she said hoping she didn't sound too sarcastic. But not really caring if she did.

"It isn't meant to be romantic. We're both attracted to each other. The media will make our lives hell no matter what the circumstances…it's rational."

"Rational? Was that what you felt last night?"

He walked around his desk in long measured strides and she fought to keep her ground. Because there was something about him that intimidated her. Something about his large frame and his stern countenance that made her want to back down. Except she didn't back down for anyone.

He put his hands on her waist, pulling her against his body. "There was nothing sensible or sane about last night. I wanted you and I didn't want to let you go without tasting your kiss at least once."

"Oh."

"I'm not romantic, Tempest. I'm a businessman and for the better part of my adult life I've been focused on only one thing."

"Ruining my father."

He nodded. He didn't even try to deny it which made her respect him just a little more.

"If we decide on an affair, don't expect romance."

"What should I expect?" she asked. No one had ever been as forthright with her as he was now. And in that moment she realized she could really fall for Gavin Renard. She realized that he was the kind of man that she'd been searching for all her life. He was solid and straight forward and he didn't care that she had more money than any one person needed.

"I'll treat you the way that you deserve to be treated in my bed and out of it."

She shivered at his words. She wanted what he'd described but if she said yes to this she'd be little more than his ornament—his date at functions until he tired of her. And a man like Gavin would tire of a woman who allowed herself to only be his bedmate.

"I want you to give me a chance to work for you, too."

He dropped his hands from her and stepped away. "I can't."

"Just let me come up with a PR plan for you. No promises of employment—just a test run to show you what I can do."

"Why is this important to you?" he asked. "You don't need the money."

"No, I don't need the money. But I want to prove to my father that he's wrong."

"What was he wrong about, Tempest?"

Me, she thought. But she'd never said that out loud in the past and she wasn't about to say it to Gavin. She didn't want him to realize that her own father thought she was little more than an ornament for men to use and display.

"That I'm not qualified to run the PR department of a large firm."

He leaned back against his desk, crossing his legs at the ankle. "Why Renard Investments?"

"Because you are rivals," she said, and then wished she hadn't.

"And that will make your success sting a little, right?"

She shook her head. "I know that makes me sound mean and petty but…"

She couldn't go on. Her father did make her want to be petty. Made her want to do ridiculous over-the-top things. Anything that would get his attention. And she was too damned old to still crave his approval. But she'd never had it and would always want it.

"It doesn't sound small at all," he said. "I imagine your relationship with your father is complicated."

"It is. What about you and Michael?"

"We're nothing like you and your dad. Michael knows that I'm here for him. So are we in agreement to an affair?"

"No."

"Why not? It's just the sort of thing you can use to get back at your father."

"He doesn't care who I sleep with."

"I'm not sure about that."

She was. "Trust me. I have it straight from the source."

He'd told her that her cheap escapades were of little consequence to him as long as she didn't bring any of the men home. And she doubted that Gavin would want to come to August's Lake Shore Drive mansion.

"He really said that to you?"

She nodded and shrugged it aside. "Let me do the PR plan…it's obvious to me that your job is your life and it will give us something to do together."

He rubbed the back of his neck. "I could never share any proprietary information with you."

It hurt a little because she knew he was trying not to say that he didn't trust her. But once he got to know her, she was sure she could change his mind.

"I can do something about your reputation as a cold-blooded shark. Someone who goes in for the kill when a company is floundering."

"I like that rep."

"Maybe I can come up with a plan to humanize you."

He stared at her for a long moment and then he shrugged. "Okay, but I'm not hiring you."

"We'll see."

Five

Tempest was thirty minutes late to her meeting with Charlie. She wasn't exactly sure of what she'd agreed to in Gavin's office but she knew they'd discuss it further when he came to her house tonight for dinner.

She called her housekeeper and informed her she'd have a guest for dinner. Then she stopped in front of the Tempest's Closet corporate offices. Since their earlier meeting at Starbucks had been delayed, Charlie had suggested they try for lunch. He was lounging against a low railing that lined the handicap ramp leading to the entrance, cigarette in one hand, cell phone in the other.

The wind blew his short hair and he stubbed out

his cigarette as he saw her. As he walked toward her, she realized that there was more to Charlie than she'd first thought. He opened the door to her Aston Martin convertible and slid onto the leather seat.

"Sorry I'm late," she said as he slid into the car. He smelled of the summer air and cigarettes. She'd quit smoking almost three years ago but she missed it.

"You're doing me a favor," he said, putting on his seat belt.

"Where to?" she asked, as she eased the car out into the light traffic. It was the middle of the afternoon so they wouldn't have to worry about the lunch crowds.

"Some place quiet so we can talk without worrying if we're overheard."

She chose a small restaurant in the Art Institute that was quiet at this time of the day. They sat in the back corner and she gave him all the information she had on the projects she'd been working on. The part that would be more difficult for Charlie would be using her contacts.

She wrapped things up quickly. "Well, that's it then. Good luck, Charlie." She put her notebook back in the large Coach bag that she'd brought with her and made a move to get up.

"Thank you, Tempest. There's one more thing," Charlie said. His tone of voice made her leery. What else could they possibly have to discuss?

"What?" she asked. She sat back in her chair

almost afraid of where this was going, which was ridiculous because Charlie had nothing over her. He had nothing she wanted, except her father's respect.

"The picture of you and Gavin Renard from today's paper."

"What about it?" She tried not to sound defensive. But she didn't think that Charlie was the right guy to be talking to her about her personal life.

Charlie glanced away from her. "Your father has made that our number one priority."

"I don't see why it's any business of his. I am no longer employed by Tempest's Closet."

"You are still a major shareholder."

Tempest rubbed the back of her neck and really wished she'd stayed in bed this morning. "I always let my father vote my shares. If he has a problem with me he knows how to reach me."

Charlie didn't say anything, just leaned back in his chair. "He's put you back on the payroll. There was an article in the business section tying your departure and your relationship with Renard together."

"No. Tell him no."

"I can't, Tempest. He's not listening to me on this subject."

"Who is he listening to?"

"I have no idea. I got an e-mail from Jean this morning and tried to call him."

Jean was her father's secretary. "I'll take care of it."

"Thanks," he said, getting to his feet. "If it turns

out you're still in my department, I'd like you to handle the new store opening in Los Angeles."

"Better have a back-up plan because I'm nothing more than a shareholder now."

"I do," he said. She followed him out of the restaurant, trying to numb her mind. But it wasn't working. Just when she thought there was no way for her to feel more insignificant to her father, he did something like this. But she'd moved on and was trying to win Gavin's trust. That meant there was no way she could return to work for Tempest's Closet.

She tried to tell herself that it didn't matter what he did, that she'd moved on. And a part of her had moved on. A big part of her was looking forward to a new relationship with Gavin and the new opportunities he offered.

Charlie said nothing as she drove him back to his building. The entire time she stewed over her father and the fact that he thought…who knew what he thought.

"I'm not coming back to work at Tempest's Closet, Charlie. As far as I'm concerned I resigned and no one from HR has contacted me."

Charlie smiled at her as he opened the door. "I understand."

"It's nothing against you," she said, realizing that he might think she'd quit because he'd gotten the promotion she wanted.

"I never thought it was. Take care of yourself."

He eased out of the car. She grabbed her cell phone

thinking she should call her father but she didn't want to give him the pleasure of doing that. Yet this was one time when she couldn't let him ignore her wishes. She dialed his office number and got Jean.

"Is my father available?" she asked.

"I'm sorry, Tempest, but he isn't. Can I take a message?"

He was playing this through third parties and she'd be happy to let him continue on that way.

"Yes, Jean, please tell my father that I'm not coming back to work for him. Also please advise the HR department to take me off the payroll."

Jean sighed. "Umm…"

"Jean, he can't rehire me without even asking me to come back to work for him."

"You have a point. I'll make sure he receives your message."

"And the HR department?"

"Yes, I'll do that, as well."

"Thanks, Jean," she said, hanging up the phone. It occurred to her that she'd probably had more conversations with Jean than her father over her lifetime. But she refused to dwell on that.

Instead she thought about the coming evening. Staying in was out of the question. She wanted to go public with Gavin in a big flashy way. In a way that would garner the attention of every media outlet. She wasn't just doing it to annoy her father, this would help Gavin, too.

* * *

Tempest e-mailed him a PR plan for changing his image within the local community. He glanced at the first few items then put the plan out of his head. He was a businessman who focused on the bottom line and didn't give a damn what anyone thought of him.

The first thing on the list was to buy art for the lobby of his building. She'd put a little smiley face after that one and a note that said just kidding.

She was the only one who did that. Joked with him, well except for his brother but that was simply because he and Michael had relied on each other and only each other for the majority of their lives.

"What's that?"

"Nothing," he said, fighting the urge to minimize his Outlook e-mail box. He hadn't heard Michael enter but then the door between both of their offices was often left open.

"Nothing?" Michael leaned over his shoulder for a closer look. "It looks like an e-mail from Tempest Lambert. I thought you said there was nothing going on with her."

"Who are you, Katie Couric?" he asked, taking the mouse from Michael's hand before he could open the e-mail.

"Ha, very funny. Why is she e-mailing you a PR plan?"

"Michael, did you come into my office for a specific reason or just to be a pain in the ass?"

"I did have a reason. Being a pain in your ass is just something I throw in for fun."

"I'm pretty sure Mom wouldn't miss you if I relocated you to our Alaskan office."

"We don't have an office in Alaska," Michael said with a small grin.

"We will if you don't get to the point."

Michael leaned against the desk, crossing his legs at the ankles and his arms over his chest. "Our inside source at Tempest's Closet said there was a lot of rumbling going on today in mid-to-executive level management. Did you know Tempest no longer works for Tempest's Closet?"

"She mentioned it." She'd come to him for a job as soon as her father had shown her the door. He was beginning to believe there was more to her unemployment than met the eye.

"Well the inside dirt is that she quit when Charles Miller was promoted to the PR vice president opening," Michael said.

Gavin leaned back in his chair away from his brother and the desk. He hadn't asked about why she'd left Tempest's Closet. Hadn't really wanted to know the details because then he might sympathize with her. Might have a real reason to trust her and then he'd have no barriers to keep between them.

"Who's Charles Miller?" he asked. He was as familiar with the Tempest's Closet organizational chart as he was with his own. He knew all the players in the company and the name Charles Miller wasn't ringing any bells.

"We're checking him out. Seems like that picture of the two of you caused a stir, as well."

He didn't give a crap what people thought about him. He had made himself stop caring the day his parents had moved them out of their large family home just off of Main Street and into a mobile home park. It was the same day that the local Tempest's Closet announced record sales and plans to double the size of their store.

But he didn't like the fact that anyone was speculating on what was between him and Tempest. What he felt for her was too raw. Too protective and possessive for him to want to share it with the world.

"We dealt with the picture, too," Gavin said, not wanting to give the situation too much weight.

"You didn't give Tempest an ultimatum, did you?" Michael asked.

"No. Why would I do that?" Then again, she'd left his office to go to a meeting. One with her father? Tempest didn't have it in her to be a corporate spy, did she?

"August wants her to come back to work for him."

Gavin didn't want to ask if she'd said yes. A minute ago he'd been certain she'd say no to anything her father asked of her. Now he wasn't. He realized steamy hot attraction and one kiss weren't nearly enough to constitute a working knowledge of her.

"Don't you want to know what she said?"

"How does your spy get this information so quickly?"

"We pay him really good money and he's highly placed."

Seriously he wondered if they had any property in Fairbanks that would make a nice office. They didn't do a lot of business in Alaska but Michael would be out of his hair for a while. "You're on my last nerve."

He chuckled. "But we're blood so you'll forgive me, right?"

He shrugged. "What'd she say?"

"She told him no."

Relief and a kind of sadness moved through him. He was glad she hadn't gone back to work for her dad but the sensitive woman he was coming to know had to have been hurt by that situation.

He would look at her PR plan and see if she really knew her stuff. If she did, maybe he'd find a way to hire her in one of their subsidiaries. She couldn't work in the corporate offices or he wouldn't get any work done from lusting over her.

"Was that it?"

"No. The Tempest's Closet stockholders are antsy and several of them put out feelers to sell blocks of shares."

Tempest had been more of a help to him than she could ever guess. Not just because she'd acted the way he'd hoped she would with her father today.

"Did you make an offer?"

"Yes, I'll know something tomorrow."

"Keep me posted," Gavin said reaching over to turn off his laptop.

"I will. Where are you going?"

"What are you my social secretary?"

"You never leave the office before eight."

"Then maybe it's time I started."

Michael didn't say anything as Gavin pulled on his coat and gathered his briefcase.

"You okay, bro?"

"Yes," he said and walked out of the office. But he wasn't so sure that he was okay. Everything in his life was changing. And it was all to do with one woman. The daughter of his enemy.

Tempest wanted nothing more than to stay in for the evening but she knew it would be construed as hiding out so she got dressed for her date with Gavin. He hadn't responded to the e-mail she'd sent him earlier. She'd left a message with his secretary letting him know that she was expected at a new club downtown later tonight.

The celebrity deejay was the brother of one of her oldest boarding school friends and she wanted to lend her support to him. But she was tired and deep inside where she didn't lie to herself she was one mass of aching hurt.

She didn't know what Gavin expected from her other than sex. She didn't know why she still allowed her father to hurt her. And she knew that going back to work for Tempest's Closet would change absolutely nothing. Her father would still treat her with the same disdain he'd held her in for her entire life.

She reached for the pitcher of margaritas that her housekeeper had left sitting on the bar. Getting drunk or a least a little buzzed seemed like just the thing to insulate her from the worries in her head and the aching loneliness in her heart.

But she thought of Dean struggling to stay sober in a safe house in Italy. And knew that too easily she could slide back into the party lifestyle that had almost killed him.

The doorbell chimed and she sank down in one of the gilt Louis XIV chairs that faced the fireplace. She set her margarita on the end table, then reconsidered, thinking it might look as though she'd been waiting desperately for him. She heard his footsteps in the hallway leading to her sitting room a second before she decided to pick up the drink. She took a sip and tried to look…

He was gorgeous. He stood in the doorway in the light of the setting sun and she forgot about the worries in the back of her mind. Forgot that she wasn't sure she trusted him. Forgot everything except the slow physical awareness that was spreading through her body.

Her pulse picked up and her breathing became a little shallower. He still wore his suit jacket but his collar was open and she saw that he didn't wear a T-shirt underneath. His skin was tan and she wondered if he was muscular. She wanted to see what was beneath that shirt.

"Good evening, Tempest," he said.

Just hearing her name on his lips was enough to make her stand up. She had to stop this. This was ridiculous. She wasn't even sure she trusted the man; was she really going to let this attraction take control of her life?

"Can I get you a drink?"

"What are you drinking?"

"Margarita."

"I'll have one."

She fixed his drink a little nervously. She knew what she wanted and had no qualms about going after it. But the scene with Charlie this afternoon when he'd told her about her dad kept replaying in her head. What if Gavin found out and thought he couldn't trust her?

She handed him the drink but his fingers lingered on hers. Trapping her hand in his grip. She glanced up at him and felt the world drop away. Felt it narrow to just the two of them. She no longer heard the sounds of Maria in the kitchen or the ticking of the grandfather clock in the hallway.

It was just her and Gavin and nothing else mattered. And she wanted life to stay that way. Suddenly it didn't seem like a good idea to go out tonight—she wanted to be all alone with this man, with no outside interference whatsoever.

"That's a big pitcher for one person."

She knew that. She'd never had a problem with alcohol so she used it when she needed to. But now that Gavin was here she realized how it might look to him. "I was hoping to have help drinking it."

"Not getting drunk?" he asked.

"I did think about it," she admitted. There were so many rumors about her that she tried to never tell lies. Not even ones that would help her.

He raised one eyebrow at her.

"It hasn't been the best day for me," she said reluctantly.

"Because of the picture?" he asked.

"Sort of." No way did she want to go into all the sordid details of her pathetic relationship with her father.

"Want to talk about it?"

"No—yes."

He drew her over to the loveseat and sat down, sprawled his large frame on the piece of furniture. It made her realize how big he was as he settled in next to her.

"Talk."

She stared up at him wishing she'd never opened her mouth. He seemed so immune to the doubts that plagued her, above such petty worries as what someone else thought of him.

"How do you do it?" she asked, taking an absent sip of her margarita.

"Do what?" He set his glass down on the table, stretching one long arm along the back of the loveseat.

She stared at his hands instead of at him. No lies, she thought. Realizing that with Gavin that rule was going to be much harder to keep. He made her feel so vulnerable and she hated that.

"Stay so cool," she said. She really wanted to know. She could fake it for a while and people never seemed to notice the falseness of her smile but inside she died a little each time. And she was so incredibly tired of feeling empty.

When she was with Gavin she felt more than she wanted to, which was a double-edged sword. She craved the attention and the emotions he effortlessly brought to the fore but at the same time she was afraid of him.

He reached for his glass and took a sip of his margarita. "I don't"

"It looks like it."

"Appearances can be deceiving."

"Yes, they can."

Tempest tried to push it from her mind but the thought weighed heavily there. Appearances could be deceiving. What was Gavin hiding, and was she really going to try to figure it out?

Six

Appearances were a tricky thing, Gavin thought as he watched Tempest move through the crowded club. Anyone seeing her now would never have guessed at the vulnerability he'd witnessed in her home earlier.

He'd ached to draw her into his arms and just hold her but he knew he was just as much to blame for her current troubles. He'd been thinking about it all night how the one that'd come out looking bad in the entire photo-lost-job situation was Tempest.

Her father had gotten the sympathetic he's-done-everything-for-her treatment and Gavin himself had gotten the businessman-led-astray-by-a-beautiful-woman thing. It wasn't fair, he thought.

But then he'd learned early on that life wasn't fair. And usually he didn't dwell on that.

She was incandescent tonight, glowing with a light from within, as she moved among her high-society friends, the groupies who followed the deejay from club to club and the paparazzi that seemed to follow her everywhere she went.

Gavin leaned against the wall in the VIP section and just watched her. He still had absolutely no idea what he was going to do with her other than take her to his bed. He knew that if he wanted her there tonight he should be a little more sociable but night-clubs like this left him cold. And pretending to be something he wasn't simply wasn't his way.

"Are you going to stand here all night?" she asked, coming up to him. Her hips moved in time with the driving beat of the music.

"Probably."

"Why?"

"This isn't my scene."

"No kidding. Why don't you give it a try?"

"I'm not really social."

"I am."

"I've noticed."

She glanced up at him. He wished he could read what was going on inside her head because he knew something was off but had no idea how to fix it.

"Why don't you like this scene?" she asked.

"There's no point to this."

"The point is to have fun…is that something you've heard of?"

"Ha, ha, smart-ass. Of course I've heard of fun, it's just so pointless to hang out in a club when you know there are people waiting to take your picture and write down everything you've done."

She pulled him further into the VIP section to a small booth in the back that was shrouded in shadows. She scooted in and then glanced up at him. "Sit down."

He slid in next to her. Giving into the temptation to put his arm around her shoulders and tug her up against the side of his body.

"Why are we back here?" he asked.

"No one can hear us back here or see us."

"If you wanted privacy, why'd we come here?"

"Because my doorman at home is on the payroll of at least two tabloid newspapers. He always tells them when I have visitors of the opposite sex and how long they stay. This way he won't have much to report."

He took a strand of her hair in his hand swirling it around his finger. "How do you stand it?"

"It's my life."

He added this complication to the matrix running in the back of his mind. It wasn't enough that she was August's daughter. She was someone who was used to living in the spotlight.

"Seriously, Tempest, how do you stand it?"

She stared down at the table. "I'm one big fraud.

I smile at strangers and chat up acquaintances and pretend that they are friends."

He heard more than her words and knew that deep inside these kinds of situations took a toll on her. And he wasn't going to add to it. He had the money and the manpower to shield her.

He let his fingers slide down her neck, tipping her head back so that she rested on his arm. He traced the lines of her face, trying to ease the stress that he saw there. Then he leaned down and brushed his lips over hers. Just felt her in his arms, where he'd wanted her since she'd left his office hours ago.

She opened her lips and he felt the brush of her tongue against his. Her hands caged his face and she lifted slightly so she was pressed more firmly against him.

Deep inside where he'd been hiding for the majority of his adult life he felt something melt. Some part of him that he planned to ignore, but all the same that part knew that this woman was his.

His.

He took control of the kiss, changing it from a sweet gentle meeting of mouths, to an all out claiming of the woman. He wanted to make sure there was no doubt in Tempest's mind that she belonged to him.

A flashbulb illuminated them and he lifted his head, pushing to his feet, but Tempest stilled him with her small manicured hand on his arm.

"Want to dance?"

"No."

"Gavin…"

He stopped walking toward the velvet ropes and the photographer who'd snapped their picture.

"What?"

"I'm sorry my life is like this."

He glanced back at her, turning to face her. "I am, too. Let's get out of here."

"I wanted one dance with you," she said.

"Ah, hell, you know that guy is still out there," he said.

"Yes, I do."

He wasn't much of a dancer but couldn't pass up the chance to hold her in his arms. She'd changed into a skirt that was so tight and short, he couldn't keep his eyes off her legs, which were long and slim, accentuated by the heels she wore.

"Why don't you have a bodyguard?"

She shrugged but he wasn't going to let her evade the question.

"Tell me," he said.

"I did have one but he worked for my father. When I left finishing school my dad and I had a falling out so he cancelled the contract with the company that provided my bodyguard. My father said if I was going to court trouble then I deserved to get myself out of it…I've just kind of never wanted to give him the satisfaction of knowing I couldn't take care of myself…so no bodyguard for me. I can handle the paparazzi without one."

"Give me a minute," he said.

"What are you doing?"

"Hiring a bodyguard. And it's not because I think you can't handle yourself."

"Why then?"

He didn't answer her, refused to say out loud that he needed to protect her. Instead he dialed the private investigating firm that he used in researching company CEOs before he decided to invest in their businesses. He had a short conversation with the owner and the promise that a bodyguard would be along shortly to ensure their privacy.

She grabbed his hand, tugging him toward the dance floor. He pulled her into his arms and realized dating this woman was more complicated than a million different mergers but that didn't deter him from going after her.

Tempest watched the street lights and shadows go by as Gavin drove. He wasn't going in the direction of her condo and she was pretty sure she was going to get an up-close and personal tour of his place.

The bodyguard he'd summoned to the club was following behind them making sure they weren't followed too closely. She wasn't sure that the press would stay away from her, but it was nice for tonight to have this sense of anonymity. It was something she'd never had

"Thanks," she said, at last. Needing to talk, needing to get out of her own head before she started crying about her life. God, how pitiful was that? She had a nice home, food in her kitchen and a roof over her head. There was nothing to be so sad about.

"For?" he asked, his voice low.

She shrugged, wrapping one arm around her waist as a chill spread through her body. "The body-guard thing."

"It was nothing. Cold?"

She shook her head but he adjusted the air conditioning making it warmer on her side. But it wasn't nothing to her. Her father always said she brought the intense scrutiny on herself. That if she'd acted like a lady they would never have been interested in her. Ironic that when she cleaned up her act and started behaving like a lady, he was the one who became more indifferent in her.

Gavin wasn't indifferent. But he was still holding a part of himself back from her. Not that she necessarily blamed him. She'd read the *Page Six* dirt on herself and knew without a doubt that anyone with a nice normal life would think twice about getting too involved with her.

But Gavin didn't have a normal life. He had a life where he was gunning for Tempest's Closet. Why? Even her father had never said exactly why.

"Can I ask you a question?" she asked into the silence. She wanted to unravel Gavin and figure out what made him tick. And a big part of who he was, according to rumor, involved the take over of her father's company.

"You just did," he said wryly.

"Are you trying to be funny?"

"I don't know, is it working?"

"No."

She turned in her seat to face him. His stark features were illuminated by the dashboard lights making him seem more of a stranger than she wanted him to be.

"Why are you fixated on taking over Tempest's Closet?"

He glanced over at her and then back to the road. "It makes good business sense."

"There seems like there is more to it than that."

He turned off the highway and entered an exclusive neighborhood. "Maybe there is."

"If you don't want to say then just tell me it's off-limits."

"I don't want to say anymore about it," he said, pulling into the garage of a large McMansion. There were two other cars parked in the three-car garage. One low, sexy sports car and an SUV that looked like it had been taken off-roading.

"Why not?"

"Tempest, it's private."

"And I'm only allowed to fall into a certain part of your life?"

He shrugged.

"I'm not into anonymous sex."

"Neither am I. I like you and I'll share parts of my life with you."

But just the parts that he wanted to share.

"I can't do this," she said. She'd had affairs in the past that were short and frivolous but she couldn't do that with Gavin. She wanted to know more about him. He made her feel safe and real.

And she was so afraid that if she slept with him, she'd be in over her head.

He glanced over at her his features illuminated this time by the garage lighting and she knew this was a crossroads for them. Either they'd continue on in a relationship or they'd part ways.

Gavin rubbed the back of his neck, He had known this moment was going to come—he should have been better prepared for it. And he'd already decided she was not a corporate spy. Was it possible that August didn't know why he was coming after him? Or was it only his daughter?

"Come inside and we can talk. If you still want to go home…I'll take you. The bodyguard is yours no matter what choice you make. Everyone deserves privacy."

"Thanks for saying that. A lot of people believe I deserve the attention. That it is some kind of punishment for my actions."

"People?"

She shrugged and he knew that she meant her father. She'd said as much earlier but now she wasn't going to say anymore. He opened his car door and pocketed his keys. He escorted her into his house.

As the door closed behind them he felt a sense of rightness. She belonged here.

He could talk her into anything on his home turf. But he didn't want to persuade her to stay. He wanted her as hot for him as he was for her.

He led her into the living room with the plasma screen TV on one wall and the tropical fish tank on the other. There was expensive art hanging on the wall that his decorator had purchased and the floor was made of marble he'd had imported from Italy. He didn't want to acknowledge it but he knew that he'd been working hard his entire life for a moment like this one.

He wanted her to know that he wasn't some poor kid who'd lost everything and lived on government subsidies. He didn't want to acknowledge that part of him, not in front of her. But he was going to have to. There was no way to talk about his focus on acquiring Tempest's Closet without talking about the past.

And standing in this opulent room even he felt the distance between who he'd been and who he was today.

"Can I get you a drink?"

"No, I'm good," she said, drifting around the room and settling on the couch.

He walked over to the well-stocked bar in the corner and poured himself two fingers of scotch before turning back toward her.

She looked like a sexy angel in the dim lighting. And he didn't want to let her go. Even though he

knew deep inside that he wasn't going to get to keep
her. The past was too much a part of the man he was
today for her to every really be a part of his life but
he wanted whatever time they had.

"Am I pushing too hard?" she asked. "I know
what it's like to feel like you're being hounded."

"Ah, honey. You humble me." And she really did.
She was selfless in a way that he knew she wouldn't
recognize. She was constantly thinking of others
and though she had a reputation for being a party-
girl and going after only what would make her feel
good, he was coming to realize that making others
feel good was what did it for her.

"Come sit with me, Gavin."

He sank down on the sofa beside her and she
turned toward him, slipping off her shoes and curling
those long legs under her. The hem of her skirt rose
to a dangerous level. He couldn't tear his gaze from
her thighs until she put her hand on his forearm.
Stroked her fingers up and down his arm.

She stared up at him with those wide-blue eyes
of hers. Seeing past the successful man he was today
and straight into the heart of him. Straight to that
little boy he'd all but forgotten about.

He tugged her into his arms, until her back rested
against his chest and she faced away from him. He
wrapped his arm around her waist and lowered his
head to the top of her hair. Breathing in that sweet
clean scent that he associated only with her.

"Tempest's Closet industries took my life from

me," he said, softly. And realized he wasn't going to be able to do this. He didn't want to sound like some kind of sap whose life was ruined. Because he really couldn't imagine living another way. He was happy being the man he was today. And grudgingly he realized he owed that to August Lambert.

"How?" she asked, tipping her head back on his shoulder. Her silky hair slid against his skin.

"The same way they did so many lives in this country. Tempest's Closet came to my home town and the small merchants in the town slowly went out of business."

"Tempest's Closet brings a lot of money into the communities that it develops in. You know a lot of local governments solicit Tempest's Closet to get them to come to their towns."

"I thought you stopped working for Tempest's Closet."

"That doesn't mean I'm not still proud of what my father has done."

He pushed to his feet and walked away from her. This wasn't something he could ignore. "For every job that Tempest's Closet brings into a community at least five are lost. And a way of life is compromised."

She sat up. "A way of life? Tempest's Closet isn't going in and making these communities into company towns that they run. They bring fashion and style to places where such things weren't even talked about before."

"We're never going to agree on this."

"I know," she said, quietly. She studied him for a long moment and then stood and walked over to him.

"Did your family lose everything?"

He nodded.

"We owned the general store. You know one of those small old-fashioned ones that carried everything from clothes to hardware to groceries."

"Tempest's Closet shouldn't have affected the hardware and grocery part of your business," she said.

"No, but the other large retailers that followed Tempest's Closet to our town did."

"I'm sorry."

"Don't be. It made me who I am."

"I like who you are," she said, wrapping her arms around his waist and resting her head against his chest.

He tugged her up against him. There was no room for any other thoughts. He didn't want to dwell on the past or think about business. He just wanted to relish the feel of her.

To focus solely on her and the now. The part of his life that she could be in. He danced her around the living room. Just enjoying the feel of her in his arms.

He lowered his head to hers and kissed her again. Rekindling the desire that was never far from the surface when she was around. She responded instantly, tipping her head back and thrusting her tongue into his mouth.

He lifted her in his arms and walked out of the living room toward the stairs and his bedroom.

Seven

Gavin's bedroom was different than she expected it to be. Done in warm earth tones with a large Ansel Adams' photograph from the Mural project but it wasn't a poster it was the real thing. She moved closer to it when he set her on her feet. The stark black-and-white photograph called to her as nothing else could.

Gavin put his hands on her shoulders and drew her back against his body. Just holding her while she examined the photograph to her heart's content. She felt the subtle movements of his body rubbing against hers. Felt his erection against the small of her back and knew in a few minutes that passion would take over and they'd be making love. But for this one moment she felt something she'd never expected to feel. Something she'd long ago given up searching for. A kind of welcome and peace.

She closed her eyes and turned in his arms, resting her head over his heart and wrapping her arms around his body. He lowered his head over the top of hers. The warmth of his breath stirred her hair before he cupped her face and tipped her head back so that their eyes met.

She tunneled her fingers through his hair, drawing his head down. Their mouths met, his lips rubbing lightly over hers. Touching her gently…so gently. She knew she'd never get enough of tasting him.

Then the dynamic of the embrace changed. His tongue thrust deep into her mouth as his hand swept down her back. He cupped her butt and drew her closer to him. His erection rubbed against her belly. She moaned deep in her throat and moved closer to him.

Her hands clutched at his shoulders, her body craving more. She felt his hands at the hem of her short skirt. Sliding up underneath it and rubbing random patterns on her skin. She shifted her legs, craving his touch higher. But he kept up the subtle caresses.

"Gavin…"

He nibbled his way from her mouth to her ear biting the lobe. When he spoke his words were a strong puff of air in her ear, felt as much as heard. "What?"

"Touch me," she said, breathing the words against his neck. Damn, he smelled so good. She wanted to close her eyes and lose herself in the sensation of him. The feel of his big hands on her skin. The white-hot tingle that followed his touch. The sweet craving for more that was permeating her bloodstream.

He moved his hand higher cupping her butt cheek and holding her in place as she undulated against him. She moaned deep in her throat, trying to stand on her toes and feel his erection where she wanted it. Needed it.

She lifted her leg trying to wrap it around his hip but he gripped her thigh in his hand, his long fingers holding her so close to where she needed his touch.

"I am touching you, Tempest."

But it wasn't enough. She shifted again in his arms but it was futile. She wasn't getting closer to him until he decided she was. "I need more."

"Not yet," he said.

She realized then that he was playing her. Not in a malicious way but in a power way. One that made her submissive to him and his desires. He'd give her what she wanted but only on his agenda. She didn't understand what his agenda was here. But she felt that he did have one.

She stepped away and looked at him. His gray eyes were cold and flat. She saw the passion in him in the flush of his skin and the erection straining against the front of his pants. But she saw that he kept a part of himself locked away from her and this moment.

"What are you waiting for?"

He reached out then, taking a strand of her hair

in his hand and drawing it through his fingers. She tipped her head toward him and his thumb found her lower lip. She knew her mouth was swollen from his kisses and it tingled as he moved his thumb over it.

"Just waiting," he said.

She couldn't follow the conversation anymore. Her world had narrowed to his hand in her hair and that thumb rubbing over her lip. She caught it gently between her teeth, sucking him deep into her mouth and his hand on her hair stilled. His eyes narrowed, his breath hissing out in a rush.

He drew her closer again, wrapping her hair around his hand. He pulled his thumb from her mouth and ran it across her lips and then down the side of her neck. He stroked her pulse there at the bottom of her neck before moving down the edge of her blouse. Caressing the skin left bare there.

His features were harsh and strained in the light, yet very sensual as he focused on touching her. And she realized what he was waiting for. He didn't want to rush this moment and neither did she.

He brought his mouth down to hers. His one hand burrowed deep in her hair, holding her still for his possession. His tongue delving deep, leaving no inch of her mouth unexplored.

His thumb stroked over her skin, down beneath the silky fabric of her summer weight top. Finding the lacy edge of her bra with his thumb, moving lower and flicking around the edge of her breast. She shivered as he came close to touching her where she needed it most. Her nipple tightened in anticipation but he just kept moving down her body. His knuckles brushing the underside of her breast.

He sucked her lower lip between his teeth and bit down delicately on her flesh before drawing his head back. "Take your top off."

She shivered again as the rough growl of his voice played over her skin. She drew her shirt up over her head tossing it to the floor.

"Now your skirt," he said.

She took a step back but his hand in her hair kept her bound to him. "Do it here."

She trembled at the command in his voice. She'd never had a man treat her this way in the bedroom. Moist heat pooled between her legs as she reached behind her back and loosened the button and then drew down the zipper. With a swivel of her hips the skirt slid down her legs and pooled at her feet.

"Now take off your underwear," he said.

She undid the bra and slid it off her arms. She leaned against him for a moment, letting the tips of her breasts brush against the crisp linen shirt he wore.

She hesitated to remove her panties. She'd be naked and he was fully clothed. He seemed to sense her hesitation and leaned down to capture her bottom lip between his teeth. He sucked on her lip until shivers ran down her body. Being naked while he was fully clothed no longer mattered. He lifted his head and she reached for her panties, sliding them slower down her legs until at her knees they fell to the floor.

Gavin stepped back to look at her. "Go lay on the bed."

In the lamp light her skin glistened and it was clear to him that she was too fine to be in his bed. In that moment, with her lying there waiting for him, he knew that he wasn't good enough for her. He was too rough—still the boy who'd had to fight for everything he owned—despite the millions he'd made.

He was too demanding and she was too…out of his league. There was the slight hint of shyness in her eyes as she settled in the center of his bed. And there was a part of him—granted it wasn't a big part—but a part of him that demanded she prove that she really wanted him.

"I'm here," she said, her voice soft and tentative. This wasn't the same nervy woman who'd confronted him in his office demanding a job.

He should walk away from her. Tell her to get dressed and make her leave. There was no good way for this to end, this affair they'd talked themselves into. His need for revenge was too great and as he looked at her lying there he wished…ah, hell, he wished he were a different man. The kind who could walk away from the past because he had a glimpse of what the future could be.

"Gavin," she said, lifting her arms toward him.

Walking away was no longer an option. Not when

she watched him with those wide vulnerable eyes and stared up at him like she really wanted him. Like her heart was empty without him. And God knew his heart was empty without her.

He sank down on the bed next to her hip, tracing the curves of her body with his hand. Her skin was porcelain and perfect. He traced a line down the center of her body over her sternum right between her two perfect breasts. Her pink nipples beaded as he moved his finger. He stopped and leaned over, breathing on her nipple, watching it tighten even more before he lowered his mouth and tasted her.

She moaned, the sound a symphony in his ears. Her hands moved restlessly, falling to his shoulders. Her nails scored his skin through the fabric of his dress shirt as she tried to draw him closer. But because he couldn't see a way to hold her in his arms forever, he wanted to make this moment last. He wanted to ensure that she never took another man to her bed and didn't think of him.

He caught her delicate flesh between his teeth as jealousy pounded through him. No other man would touch this woman the way Gavin would. His hands slid down her body gripping her hips as they lifted toward him. He pinched her other nipple and heard her gasp as he did so.

He lifted his head, making sure she was with him. She drew his head back to her breast. Lifting her shoulders so that the tight bud of her nipple brushed against first his cheek then his lips.

"More," she said.

He lowered his head to oblige her, working her nipple with his lips, teeth and tongue until her legs were moving restlessly on the bed. His body was so tight, so aching for the sweet release that she promised, that his entire being echoed with his own heartbeat.

He felt the blood pounding beneath the surface of his own skin. Felt the pulse pounding at the base of his spine and in the flesh between his legs. He attended her other nipple and then nibbled his way down her body, lingering over her flat stomach. He sucked the skin around her belly button and delighted when he skimmed his fingers lower to find the moist proof of her desire for him.

He traced the edge where the smooth skin met her curls and then ran his finger up one side of her and then down the other. The small bud in the center of those two lips was red and swollen, begging for his touch. But he ignored it. Shifting to his knees, he pushed her thighs apart.

She let them fall open making room for him between her legs. He looked down at her. Her skin was flushed with a slight pink tinge. She held her breath, everything in her body tensing as he lowered his head between her legs. Her hips rose toward him as he reached down and licked her once.

The taste of her was addicting. He pulled the flesh into his mouth, careful to treat her delicately.

She grabbed his head, pulling him against her as her hips rose with each tug of his mouth.

He bent lower to taste her more deeply. She was delicious and he knew that he'd never forget the sensations of this moment for as long as he lived.

She moaned and said something—perhaps his name or a demand—but he was lost in a red haze. He was surrounded by her and he could think of no other place he wanted to be.

He could feel her body starting to tighten around his tongue, and shifted back to see her at this moment. He wanted to watch her face as she went over the edge.

This was something that her money couldn't buy and her family name couldn't control. This was about Tempest and Gavin, he thought. He relished the sound of their names linked in his mind.

He pressed one finger inside her, then added a second finger, pushing deep and finding that spot that would bring her the most pleasure. He leaned down over her, taking her nipple in his mouth again, sucking her deep into his mouth.

She was panting, his name falling from her lips in between pleas that made no sense. He drew her out until finally he touched that bud between her legs and brought her to climax. She called his name and grasped his head, holding him to her like she'd never let go.

Shivers still rocked her body as she came back into herself. She couldn't believe Gavin was still fully dressed from the fine linen shirt down to his wingtips.

She shifted on the bed, reaching for him to draw

him down to her. He hesitated for a second and she wondered what was going on in his mind. She knew there was more to this than simple lust. Oh, God, please let it be more than lust.

She'd never had a man make her forget…forget everything except him. In the past sex was something she'd had because it was convenient or expected. But this was the first time in her life that she was with a man just because she wanted to be with him.

For the first time who she was—Tempest Lambert—was actually a strike against her. And he still wanted her.

She felt tears sting the back of her eyes and she turned her face against his chest, reaching for the buttons of his shirt. She undid them slowly, taking her time, revealing the masculine chest slowly.

Gavin wasn't waxed; she doubted it would even occur to him to do something like that. And she liked the feel of his chest hair against her fingers. She slipped her hand under the shirt and found his flat nipples. His breath caught as she scraped her nail over his flesh. She knew he wanted her.

She could feel him straining toward her through the clothing. It was a costume he wore, a façade of sophistication. She realized the real man beneath the clothing was rougher, needier and not at all sophisticated.

That very realization was exciting. She slid the shirt off his shoulders and pushed him back toward the headboard. She wanted to take her time and explore him. She wished she was brave enough to order him to take off his clothes and lay on the bed. But she wasn't.

"Why are you staring at me?"

She shook her head. No way was she going to say what she was really thinking. "You're gorgeous."

"Ha. I think we both know I'm not model material."

"No, you're not," she agreed. Because she'd been with model-type men. Men who were too picture perfect to be true. But there was something so real about Gavin. Something that made her feel real by association.

"You should at least have argued."

"Models aren't real," she said, tracing the delineated pectoral muscles on his chest. "They are airbrushed perfection."

She bent to taste his skin, licking a path over his chest. He tasted salty and his skin was warm and she closed her eyes wanting to lose herself in him again.

He turned in her arms, pinned her under his body. His mouth found hers, his tongue thrusting deep inside. The feeling of his muscled chest against her breasts was exquisite.

He reached between their bodies and freed his erection. She felt the scrape of his belt against her inner thigh as he pushed his pants down.

He hesitated as he was about to enter her body. "Are you on the pill?"

It took a second for her to understand what he was

asking. She just wanted him to drive into her and take her. Birth control. She'd never thought of the consequences of making love before…not really. But suddenly, staring up at his face in the dim lamp light, she did. She'd always vaguely wanted a family. A real family and kids. She bit her lower lip.

"Tempest?"

"No. I'm not on the pill. I'm not as promiscuous as the tabloids make me seem."

He cupped her face in his hands, leaning forward to kiss her. "I know."

Those few words made her wish they were different people. Or maybe that she was a different woman. One who would be strong enough to pull Gavin off his quest for revenge because deep inside she sensed that he'd never give up going after her father for her.

He kissed her so tenderly before moving away to put on a condom. He came back down on top of her and she put her hands on his chest, holding him back from entering her body.

Bending down, he captured the tip of her breast in his mouth. He sucked her deep in his mouth, his teeth lightly scraping against her sensitive flesh. His other hand played at her other breast, arousing her, making her arch against him in need.

"Now, Gavin. I can't wait."

"Not yet."

She reached between them and took his erection in her hand, bringing him closer to her. Spreading her legs wider so that she was totally open to him. "I need you now."

He lifted his head, the tips of her breasts were damp from his mouth and very tight. He rubbed his chest over them before sliding deep into her body.

She wanted to close her eyes as he made love to her. To somehow keep him from seeing how susceptible she was to him, but subterfuge had never been one of her strong suits. Gavin was essential to her in ways she was only beginning to comprehend.

She slid her hands down his back, cupping his butt as he thrust deeper into her. Their eyes met. She felt her body start to tighten around him, catching her by surprise. She climaxed before him. He gripped her hips, holding her down and thrusting into her two more times before he came, loudly calling out her name.

Disposing of the condom, he pulled her into his arms and tucked her up against his side.

She wrapped her arm around him and listened to the solid beating of his heart. She wanted to stay here forever wrapped in his arms. He made her feel safe and complete and she wished he didn't. She felt vulnerable to someone other than her father and that made her angry because until this moment, she'd been able to keep moving on and never look back. But now she was going to be looking back.

She understood Gavin so much better now than she ever could have before. And because she had her own weaknesses, she didn't want him to feel vulnerable with her. Plus, he had given her back something she wasn't sure she could have found on her own.

"Are you sleeping?" he asked.

She felt the vibration of his words in his chest and under her ear. She shifted in his embrace, tipping her head so she could see the underside of his jaw.

"No." This had been one of the most tumultuous days of her life. She felt that if she went to sleep she might wake up and find out that Gavin had really washed his hands of her and this had all been a dream.

"Thanks for taking care of the birth control. To be honest I wasn't thinking of anything but you," she said.

"You're welcome." He pulled her closer in his arms. "I want to take care of you, Tempest. To watch over you."

His words warmed the long cold part of her soul. And she knew then that she was starting to fall for him. How stupid was that? She'd spent her entire life trying to win her father's love and she was falling for the one man who'd make his acceptance an impossibility.

She propped herself up on his chest, looking down at him in the shadowy night. He made her feel safe and she knew it wasn't an illusion. He'd provided her a bodyguard and he held her in his arms tonight. She'd seen the same thing with his brother. The way he always protected those around him. What had happened to make him do that?

"What are you thinking about?"

"The way you take care of me. No one has ever..." she trailed off as she realized how vulnerable those words made her.

He slipped on a condom and rolled over so that she was under him. Her legs parted and he settled against her. His arms braced on either side of her body. He caught her head in his hands and brought his mouth down hard on hers. When he came up for air long minutes later, he said, "I will always."

She believed him. Gavin wasn't the kind of man to make promises lightly. When he gave his word he kept it and she wondered if she should ask him how he felt about her. If he thought he could ever love her enough to give up his vendetta against her father. But those kinds of words weren't easy to find and she was much too scared to find out that he couldn't love her to ever say them aloud.

Instead she lifted her hips toward his and felt him slip inside her body. Their eyes met and held again as he took her.

Eight

Tempest glanced at the alarm clock, afraid to move in case she woke Gavin. The illuminated dial read 2:30. She had always been a bit of an insomniac.

She felt too vulnerable lying naked in his arms. She'd shown him too much of who she really was and now he had the power to hurt her. Really hurt her and she wasn't sure she trusted him not to. Oh, he wouldn't do it intentionally. He was too caring to deliberately hurt her but she was still…afraid. She tipped her head back, staring at his beard stubbled jaw in the dim light of the moon. She wanted to touch him. To explore him now that he was sleeping and not watching her. She wanted to memorize all the little details of his body so that she'd be able to pull them out later when she was alone and remember them. So that any time she saw him at social functions she'd have a secret knowledge of the man beneath the suit. The man behind the image.

Turning in his arms she reached up and touched his jaw. She ran her finger along the edge of it and felt his breathing pattern change. She closed her eyes and held herself still. She didn't want to disturb him, wake him up and maybe remind him that she wasn't supposed to spend the night with him.

What if he asked her to go? To be honest it had happened before and nothing made her feel worse than having to put her clothes on in the middle of the night and leave. But everything with Gavin had been different. Please, God, let things still be different.

"What are you thinking about?" he asked, his voice a sleepy rumble.

"Nothing," she said, softly.

"You're tense."

"I am," she said. No point in lying.

"Why?"

She struggled not to smile. There was no artifice in Gavin. He had no time for small talk and always cut to the chase.

She shrugged, very aware that she didn't want to reveal anything else to him.

He cupped her jaw and tipped her head back so that their eyes met. In the dim light it was easy to pretend that she saw something more in his eyes than was probably there. She wanted to believe that she really did see caring, affection and then the narrowing of his eyes and lust. But she didn't want to deceive herself.

"Tell me."

"It's nothing and everything," she said. There was no other way to say it.

He shifted on the bed, pushing the pillows behind his back against the headboard and drawing her into his arms. She liked that feeling that came as she lay there. It was safety and security but more than that it was belonging. However false it might be, for this night she belonged in Gavin's arms. And there was no place she'd rather be.

"Tell me the everything part."

"I don't sleep much at night. Never have. So that's the everything. Just my normal habits."

"Why don't you sleep?"

She shrugged, reluctant to tell a bold-faced lie and say she didn't know. Her therapist and she had gone over every detail of why she didn't sleep for years. Tracing it to the night her mother had died. Being woken up by her nanny in the middle of the night and informed that her mother was asking for her. Being rushed down the hall to her parent's big dark bedroom to hold that cold limp hand. Her father sitting in one corner not even glancing in her direction, while the machines made scary noises. The nanny watching her as if she knew more than she would tell.

"Why, Tempest?"

"My subconscious thinks bad things happen at night but I want to focus on now."

"Tonight?"

"Yes, just tonight. You and I together," she said. The words should be a reminder to her that she and Gavin didn't have forever.

"We don't have much in common," he said.

She'd like to pretend that the comment was apropos of nothing but she knew he was trying to warn her in his own way that this couldn't last. She knew that she should try to guard her heart but was very afraid that it was too late.

"I don't know about that," she said, so very afraid that he was going to use that as a reason to never see her again. She didn't want that to happen. She no longer cared if she got a job at his company, just wanted to stay with him. To have a legitimate reason to stay in his life.

"Name one thing we have in common."

"We travel in the same social circles."

He tightened his arm around her shoulder. "Yeah, but I'm a fraud there. I don't belong in high society."

"You aren't a fraud, Gavin. You earned your place in that circle. So many just find themselves there because of the circumstances of their birth." People like her. If anyone was a fraud, she knew it was her. She'd spent the first part of her adult life being exactly the kind of thoughtless heiress that gave the wealthy set a bad name.

He tipped her head back and leaned down to kiss

her. It was a sweet kiss that demanded nothing and gave everything. "You've paid a high price because of the circumstances of your birth."

"So have you," she said, shifting in his arms. Turning more fully into his embrace.

He lifted his head staring down at her and she realized they both had this in common. This past shaped by their parents. Those long ago events shaping the people they were today.

He lowered his head again. This time his kiss was demanding. She tried to caress him, to draw him over her, but he held her hands in his grip. He lifted her onto his lap and he pulled her hands up behind his neck. She let him. She hung there in his embrace, letting him control her. Hoping that he'd take her again and give her the release she desperately needed to find in his arms.

Tempest was exhausted and totally able to sleep now but didn't want to miss a moment of this night. Her skin felt as if she'd been branded by him. There was beard burn on her breasts and her neck. She fingered the base of her neck where he'd sucked on her skin the last time they'd made love.

She'd never had a man so obsessed with her body. Even now while he was sleeping his hands moved down her back. Tracing the curve of her hip and then moving slowly back up. She was drowning in a sea of sensation and didn't care to be rescued.

She'd never realized how alone she'd been surrounded by the hoards of people that populated her life. But she had been lonely and it was only now that she recognized it.

"Baby, go to sleep," he said.

His voice was a deep husky murmur that made her toes curl in a good way. She lifted her thigh over his legs, curling herself around him. More fully into his arms and into his embrace.

She felt him stir against her and shifted her hips to rub against him. He rolled her under his body, taking her wrists in his hands and stretching her arms up above her head.

"What is it?" he asked.

She stared up at him, his features barely illuminated in the dim light. She ached—pleasantly from the hours she'd spent in his arms, but inside she still craved more. She had no words for what she wanted. For what it was that was keeping her from drifting to sleep.

Instead she lifted herself up, leaning on her elbow and tracing his features in the dim light. He lay still under her and let her explore. He wasn't like the pretty boys she'd grown up with. The soft boys who'd matured into fine-looking men who graced the pages of fashion magazines and society gossip columns.

He had a scar in the middle of his left eyebrow. She traced it over and over again with her finger before bending down to brush her lips over it. She found another small scar just under his left eye and then further down on his jaw and neck. "What happened?"

"Skateboarding accident."

"Skateboarding?" she asked, shifting around to rest her arms on his chest. It was the least likely thing. She couldn't picture him doing anything other than running a multi-million dollar investment group.

"I didn't grow up in a bubble."

"I know. But skateboarding?"

"Yeah, I liked it. Skateboarders don't care about anything but your board and your skills."

He didn't say anything else but she sensed there was more to it then that. She let her mind roam over what he said and suddenly it came to her. "Is that when you realized that you could make your own dynasty?"

He shifted under her, pulling her over him like a blanket and then rolling her under him.

"I'm not into dynasty building."

He wouldn't be. Not with his quest for revenge. Revenge was focused on the past. On avenging wrongs done a long time ago. Dynasty building required a forward vision—something she realized that Gavin didn't have. "Don't you think it's time you started looking to the future?"

He took her wrists in his hands and stretched her arms over his head. Pushed one thigh between her legs until he nestled between hers. Then he held her under him.

"A future with you?" he asked.

She turned her gaze from his. She hadn't been fishing for that and wasn't even entirely sure they could have something permanent together. "I don't know. I just know that you're not happy living the way you have been."

"And my happiness matters to you?"

A day ago she would have said no. That it didn't. He was just a means to an end. A way of striking back at her father. But lying with him naked in his bed having been in his arms and felt the protectiveness that was so much a part of his nature, she knew that his happiness did matter. It mattered more than she wished it did.

She tried to free her hands, wanting to touch him but he held her in an unbreakable grasp.

"Tempest, I asked you a question."

She bit her lower lip. "Yes, your happiness matters to me. Don't ask me anything else, Gavin. A man afraid of the future won't like my answer."

"I'm not afraid, honey."

He lowered his mouth to hers. His kisses overwhelmed her. They should both be sated and not interested in making love again.

Yet as he thrust his tongue deep in her mouth, she felt the rekindling of her own desire. She wanted him again. She tried to angle her head to reciprocate, he held her still.

This was his embrace and she felt the fierce need in him to dominate her here. God, he made her feel like she belonged to him. She tried to remind herself that Gavin had made her no promises, but his body moving over hers felt like a promise.

Nine

Waking in Gavin's arms wasn't something she was used to. Even after two months of quasi-living together on weekends and even during the week once and a while, she was afraid to open her eyes each morning. Afraid that somehow the relationship with him was another fantasy like the vivid dreams she sometimes had of her mother.

But the big warm hand drifting down her back and drawing her more fully against him wasn't a lie. She opened her eyes and realized that once again she was on top of him.

"Sorry," she said, trying to shift to his side.

"No problem," he said, holding her in place.

He stroked her back and shoulders until she relaxed against him. "Is this normal for you?"

She shook her head, refusing to look at him. The comforting sound of his heart beat under her ear. She wasn't sure she could explain to him why she always ended up on top of him during the night. She only knew that…heck, it felt more real when she held on to him.

"You're not exactly normal for me," she said, softly.

"Good."

She leaned up on her elbows again and noticed he was smiling. He rarely smiled, something she'd observed over the last few months but this morning he seemed…happy, content and she liked to think she had a lot to do with that.

"I'm starting to receive invitations for the fashion shows in New York next month. Do you want to go with me?"

"No."

"It would be a nice getaway."

"I can't. I have a project at work that I'm hoping to close then."

"What project?" she asked He never talked about work, which she suspected was because he was in a fierce competition with her father to take over Tempest's Closet.

"A big one."

"Involving Tempest's Closet?"

He rolled to his side, dumping her on the bed and sitting up. "I don't want to discuss it with you."

She bit her lower lip knowing she should just let it go, but the thing was they couldn't move forward as they were. They were lovers and the world knew it. The tabloids had taken to labeling her the high-society mistress. Sleeping with her father's fiercest competitor. And in essence that was true but she felt like there was so much more between the two of them.

"I think we have to." The last thing she wanted was to force this confrontation but she felt like his business with her father was always between them. It was the reason why the press were so interested in them as a couple. The reason why he wouldn't hire her at his company. The reason they lived together in a seclusion of sorts.

"Are you threatening me?" he asked, his voice a low rumbled.

Never, she thought. She was way too afraid to lose what she'd found with him. But she'd been operating on a level of fear for most of her life. All of her relationships had always been driven by that fear and she hated that. Everything about Gavin had been different and this had to be too. She took a deep breath.

"No. That would be silly. How could I possibly threaten you?"

"You have something I want very badly."

"What?" she asked, aching inside at the thought of what he might say.

She knew that Gavin wanted her in stark physical

terms. He told her every night. But she…oh, man she'd been hoping there was something more between them. Something…

And to be perfectly honest no one had ever wanted anything she had but her father's money. Oh, God, don't let him say her shares in Tempest's Closet. She thought she'd wither and die on the spot if he said that.

"Your body."

Oh, that hurt. It really did. In a way she hadn't anticipated. And now she felt small and alone. Where just a few minutes ago she'd felt powerful and sexy and wanted.

"I'm sure you can find another lover."

She wrapped her arms around herself wishing she could curl into a ball and disappear. Why exactly did she decide she wasn't running anymore? She'd had some brief thought that he was different. But this felt so painful and very familiar.

"Not like you."

She glanced up at him. "I don't want to fight but I think we need to find a way to move past your business with Tempest's Closet or else…"

"Are you going to ignore what I just said?"

"I don't know how to take that."

"You make me want to be a different man, Tempest. I wish there were a way for me to give up this thing with Tempest's Closet but it has shaped my life for too long."

She nodded understanding. Her outrageous press antics had been the same kind of thing. But she liked the life she'd made for herself once she'd stopped behaving that way. "The past is going to suck you down and leave you with nothing. You have to move on."

"I thought you said you liked who I was?"

"I do. But this thing with Tempest's Closet is…"

"Is what? We're having an affair."

She gave him a hard look. "Fine."

She turned and walked away going into the bathroom and turning on the shower. How could she have read him so wrong? How could she have misjudged the man he was? How could she possibly go back out there and face him without giving him a good piece of her mind?

There was rap on the bathroom door. Gavin entered, looking tired. The stubble on his chin darkened his features and made him seem almost menacing.

"I'm not good with this kind of thing."

"Let me take a shower and get dressed. Then we can talk."

He nodded and turned to walk out, stopping on the threshold. "I don't want to lose you."

Gavin's housekeeper Mrs. Stanton had Sundays off, which usually didn't bother him. He liked having the time alone with Tempest since she had started spending the weekends at his house. But this morning when things were so screwed up and he had no idea what to say to make them right he wished Mrs. Stanton were here.

Since she wasn't he busied himself making coffee and breakfast for Tempest. Cooking wasn't something he'd ever learned to do. He could work a grill and a microwave but breakfast wasn't exactly grilling time. Luckily Mrs. Stanton had left a breakfast casserole and some fresh fruit already cut-up in a bowl.

He put the casserole into the oven and tried not to dwell on the fact that he was losing Tempest. It was inevitable that she'd start to want more than he could give her. But then again he'd always been a hollow shell inside. The only time he didn't feel empty was when he was at work, and that had never bothered him before.

He suspected that Michael knew this, and that was why his brother spent so much of his time trying to involve Gavin in outside activities. Anything to get him away from the office.

Hell, he thought rubbing the back of his neck. He prayed that those few words he'd given her before he'd left the bathroom would be enough.

But he knew they'd held a tinge of desperation. How could Tempest miss it?

He turned on the music, filling the house with sound so he wouldn't feel so alone. But the Beastie Boys didn't work their usual magic. Didn't energize him and make him feel unbeatable. The music just made him realize how alone he truly was as he stood on the oriental carpet in the family room and stared at the electronics equipment that any man would envy.

He glanced around his opulent house. Seeing the things—instead of people—in his life. Even Michael was rarely a guest here. His mother had never visited him here. This was his inner sanctum. The place he hid from the world and ah, hell, he really couldn't imagine the place without Tempest.

He saw the ghost of her curled up on the couch next to him as he'd watched the basketball game last night. He heard her laughter in the hallway leading to the kitchen when he checked on their breakfast. He smelled that unique scent that was only Tempest. That blend of expensive one-of-a-kind French perfume and something else that was just Tempest.

He glanced over his shoulder to the other doorway and saw her standing there. Her hair was perfectly styled, her makeup flawless. She had on a pair of capri pants, a scoop neck sleeveless summer top and stylish sandals. She was the picture of casual glamour standing there.

And he saw them both clearly. Him with his stubbled jaw wearing only his boxers. Her so clearly perfect….

There might be a reason why he couldn't find the words to make her stay.

"I'd kill for a cup of coffee," she said.

She was trying for sassy but the sadness in her eyes made it impossible to pull off. He realized then that this was going to be his gift to her—this hollow emptiness he brought to all of his relationships.

Some gift. One that she'd remember long after he'd left her life. And he didn't want that for Tempest.

She should be sassy and happy. Teasing and laughing the way she'd been with him every morning until this one. But he didn't know if he could give her what she wanted.

"Gavin?"

He shook his head and pulled down the coffee mugs she'd bought for them at Starbucks, after insisting that using his company logo mugs wasn't going to cut it. They were big cups since they'd both discovered that neither of them could face the day without an extra-large-extra-strong brew. The green background with white flowers always reminded him of Hawaii.

He poured her a cup, added a splash of fat-free half and half and handed it to her. He poured his own and left it black.

"Breakfast should be ready in thirty minutes. Want to go out on the patio?"

She nodded and followed him outside. He sat down on the double-lounger and drew her down beside him. She held her coffee mug in both hands and took a tentative sip before tipping her head back against his shoulder.

She sighed but didn't say anything. His confidence rose a little when he heard that sound. She wanted to stay here with him, too. Maybe they were both in unchartered waters.

He'd always disliked August Lambert, okay, he'd

actively hated the man for years but at this moment he wasn't thinking of the past. He wanted to keep business matters out of this embrace and not let work affect his time with her.

He put his coffee mug on the table next to him and took hers and did the same. He turned and pulled her flush against his body.

She wrapped her arms around his neck and pulled herself closer to him. He held her in his arms hoping this would be enough. Hoping that somehow she'd be able to determine from his embrace that he needed her in his house, needed her in his bed, needed her in his life. Only now, when he felt like he might lose her, did he realize how intensely he wanted to keep her here.

"I can't say the words you want me to."

"I don't know what words I want you to say."

"Something about giving up going after your father's company."

She shrugged but he saw in her eyes that he was right. "Why can't you give it up?"

He didn't want to talk about that but he saw in her eyes that she did need the words and if she were any other woman he'd say "screw it" and walk away. Instead he sat up and grabbed his coffee mug, using the drink as a distraction until he could figure out what to say.

Tempest watched Gavin as he pushed to his feet and paced around the patio. A part of her really wanted to just let this go. She was used to taking only what the men in her life wanted to give her. Scrambling around for any bit of attention and then gratefully basking in it until they tired of her and moved on.

But she couldn't do that with Gavin. She was falling for him. Who was she kidding—she was already in love with him. He was the kind of man she'd always wanted in her life.

So why the hell didn't she just keep her mouth shut and let things ride? Mind her own business about the Tempest's Closet takeover, hard as it might be. She shook her head and reached for her coffee mug. Taking a small sip, she realized that settling with Gavin wasn't enough. She'd never really loved any of the men she'd been involved with before. She loved Gavin and that made all the difference. She didn't want to be a tabloid footnote to the merger or takeover with Tempest's Closet. They needed to clear the air about it to stand a chance of staying together.

"Gavin?"

He cursed under his breath and turned back to her. He watched her carefully and she saw him searching for the right words to say. That gave her hope as nothing else could. He wanted this relationship between them to work, too.

"I don't want to talk about business with you," he said.

Was it really just business? She doubted it since he'd brought it up this morning. From the beginning of their relationship he'd been careful to avoid conversations about her time at Tempest's Closet and he never talked about his own work, except to continue to turn her down when she asked him to hire her. To be honest she'd pretty much given up working for him.

"I don't think this is about Renard Investments and Tempest's Closet. There's so much more going on here than that."

"Yes, there is. But it's personal. And I don't want you to know that side of me."

She saw the concern in his eyes. The anger and the fear. Did he really think that hearing him admit to things she already suspected would make her leave?

"I'm not going to look at you differently."

"You will."

His confidence shook her own and she worried about what he might say. Maybe this would be the morning he walked out of her life. Oh, God, she really hoped it wasn't.

"Just say it. Don't worry about how it sounds, just say it."

He ran his hand through his hair and then sat down in one of the arm chairs across from her. He was muscled and lean sitting there looking for all the world like a man who had it all. The kind of man who clearly could have anything he wanted because he wasn't afraid of hard work.

"I want revenge on your father."

"Revenge?" She'd guessed there was something more to the take-over than just business. But revenge?

"Yes."

"Why?"

"He took everything from us. And I want to do the same to him."

"Does your family feel that way, too?"

"My mother doesn't. But Michael does."

Of course his mother wouldn't. A mother would know that revenge was too destructive. A mother would weep for her son and the fact that he could never have a future without letting go of the past.

Tempest felt a knot of ice form in her stomach. She'd expected something tied to pride. Something that she could combat. Something that she could find a way to fix so that they could be together.

"Tempest, just know…I wish it were different."

She saw him then. Heard the rap music still pulsating from the stereo in the family room. Saw the beautiful but empty house and the lush retreat he'd created for himself. And she sensed that he didn't know any other way to be. That he'd spent his entire life focused on one thing.

Taking over her father's company. Ruining her father. Her heart ached because her father was just like Gavin. He lived for his business, nothing could interfere with Tempest's Closet as far as August was concerned. Certainly not her.

But from the beginning Gavin had always had time for her. Granted she'd arrived in his life amid scandal but he'd always been there for her. She thought of all the things he'd done for her and how he'd filled her life in ways she'd never expected another person to.

She wasn't going to walk out on him now. She put her coffee mug down and went over to him. Sitting down on his lap she wrapped her arms around his shoulders and tucked her head under his chin.

His arms came around her and he held her so close and so tight that she knew her instincts were right. Gavin wasn't playing with her to get at her father. She imagined at first he'd had some sort of intent to that end but not now. He held her with the same intensity that she was holding him.

Both of them needed each other in a significant way. Maybe in a way he hadn't experienced before. Or allowed himself to experience before.

"There's only one question I need answered," she said, turning things over in her head until she had the kind of sharp clarity that made all the inconsequential stuff drop away.

"What is it?"

She tipped her head back and looked up into his diamond hard gray eyes.

"Do you want me to stay with you?"

"Hell yes."

"I need a commitment from you, Gavin. More than this temporary arrangement."

He buried his head in her neck and didn't say anything for a long time.

"Gavin?"

"I'm giving you more than I've ever given another woman. Can't that be enough?"

She thought about it, wanting to say yes of course she'd take whatever he had to give her. But she knew that once she started settling she'd never be able to convince him that she was worth more. That *they* were worth more.

"No, it's not."

He lifted his head, looking down at her with those startling gray eyes of his. "I don't know how to build anything," he said.

She knew that. Had seen the truth in those words more times than she'd wanted to count. "I do."

"I'll try," he said, as his mouth captured hers in the kind of kiss that left no room for thinking about anything other than Gavin.

Ten

Michael stood in the doorway leading between their offices, clearly excited about the report he held in his hands. But this was a moment that Gavin had come to dread in his mind. He knew that it was only a matter of time until August over-extended himself far enough that Renard would be in a position of power. A position that they'd maneuvered and planned to be in for over ten years, one which would enable Renard Investments to come in and take over the company.

It was what he'd focused on for years, but now that he had Tempest in his life, he was no longer confident that it was going to bring him the same sense of pleasure he'd expected it to.

"He did it. Took the bait just like you said he would. Tempest's Closet is most definitely over-extended. I just got off the phone with Hugh Stephens in Orlando. He's going to make the loan offer."

"Great." Hugh Stephens worked for one of Renard Investments subsidiaries that was connected through so many other companies that the trail was hard to trace. And knowing how desperate August's finances were as he clung to old ways of doing business, Gavin's gut had said that Hugh could get Lambert to commit to another loan. This was the final nail in the financial coffin that Tempest's Closet had been heading toward for a long time.

"Great? What the hell's going on? You've been planning this since we opened our doors and all you have to say is 'great'?"

"It's business, Michael. We knew he'd make too many mistakes eventually and Tempest's Closet would be ours. I'm not going to dance around the office."

"Given that you can't dance that's not surprising. But something's off here, bro. I figured you'd be breaking out that bottle of scotch you've kept in the wet bar for years. This is the moment we've been working for."

"I'm happy."

"But not like I thought you would be. If this isn't enough for you, what are we going after next?"

"We'll find another company that needs us."

"Gav, talk to me."

Gavin rubbed the back of his neck and refused to look at his brother. Was he having some kind of meltdown? Was he really letting a woman affect him this deeply? Did he honestly think he had any kind of control over what he felt for Tempest?

"Hell, I'm ecstatic, Michael, you know that. Let's open the Glenlivet and drink up."

Michael smiled at him and Gavin realized that his brother had been waiting for this moment for a long time, too. That even though Michael always seemed so open and jovial a part of him was waiting for this retribution against the man and the company that had so altered the course of their lives.

He poured two fingers of scotch into both of their glasses and turned to face his brother. They looked into each other's eyes. Michael's were the same deep brown that their father's had been and for a moment Gavin stood frozen in time.

He remembered what his father said all those years ago—the Renard boys were wily as foxes and twice as smart as the competition.

Michael's mind must have gone down a similar path because he said, "To the Renard boys—"

"Wily as foxes—"

"Twice as smart as the competition."

They clinked their glasses together and each of them swallowed the scotch. Gavin savored the feel of it burning down the back of his throat.

There was a knock on his office door and he

glanced at his watch. He was having lunch with Tempest today.

Just the thought of her standing on the other side of the door tinged his happiness with something sour. He put his glass down and excused himself from his brother. He opened the door and she smiled up at him.

"You ready?"

"Not yet."

"No problem. I'll just sit out here and wait for you."

But he didn't want to discuss the take-over of her father's company with his brother while she sat in his outer office.

"Michael, can we talk about this after lunch?"

Michael's shrewd gaze didn't waver as he put his glass on the counter of the wet bar. "Sure thing, bro."

"Hey, Michael. I'm going to fashion week next month, do you think your girlfriend Melinda will want to join me?" Tempest asked.

"What is fashion week?" Michael asked.

"You're kidding right?"

"No. I'm not. Will Melinda know what it is?"

Tempest and his brother continued to banter back and forth about fashion and men's ignorance of such things as Gavin turned back to his desk and logged off the network.

It felt strange to know that the end of his quest to take over Tempest's Closet was in sight. That finally the company that he'd lusted after for all these years was going to be in his hands.

Tempest's cell phone rang and she excused

herself to take the call, going out of his office. Michael closed the door behind her, pivoting to face him.

"Have you changed your mind about Tempest's Closet?"

The question was unexpected coming from Michael. "Why would you think I have?"

"Because if we go through with this take-over you're going to be destroying the company that her father named after her."

"August barely pays any attention to her."

"It doesn't change the fact that he's her father."

"My personal life is none of your business. Our company is doing what we do best. We've found a shaky investment and we're going to ride in and rescue it from failure. The investors will be happy."

Michael nodded and walked toward his own office, pausing in the doorway to glance back at him.

"Sounds perfect, Gav. Really it does, but you and I both know that nothing is perfect."

"What's your point?"

"I don't think you're going to be as happy about this as you've always thought you would be."

"I'm not the only one who wanted it."

"I know. I'm not saying this is only about you, but I do think you've changed. And taking over Tempest's Closet has never been my goal."

"The hell it hasn't. You just toasted his downfall the same as I did."

"You're right. But when Tempest walked in, I

realized that no matter what we do we are never going to get Dad back. He's dead and maybe it's time we started thinking about living our own lives."

Michael walked away and Gavin just watched him leave. Those words lingered in his ears as he stepped into the outer office and saw Tempest smile up at him. He didn't want to sacrifice his chance to have a life with her.

Gavin was too quiet during the lunch. It had been two long weeks since that morning on his patio where they'd had that tentative talk. She'd been careful of everything she said to him. Trying to keep the peace and hoping that maybe they really were building toward a life together.

But something was off today. She didn't know what it was. Maybe it was the whole fashion week thing. It was kind of silly and kind of frivolous but she loved it. It was one of the few memories she had of her mother. Even though Tempest was supposed to be in school in October her mother would always pull her out and take her to New York for the week.

They'd stay at the Plaza hotel back when it used to be a hotel. She smiled to herself. Then glanced across the car to Gavin's harsh features. She put her hand on his thigh.

"Are you upset that I brought up fashion week?" she asked, as they drove back to Gavin's office.

"Why would I be? I know that it's something

you've been planning on. I'm sure Melinda will be thrilled to go with you if she can get the time off."

"I know but it can be kind of…I don't know…trivial."

"Considering you've been talking about trying to write for *Vogue* I think it would be foolish to skip going. Have you heard back from that editor?"

The relief she felt unnerved her. Maybe it was because he'd been so quiet during lunch and she had the impression that his silence had to do with her.

"Yes. She wants me to write an article on Tempest's Closet and its tradition of bringing haute couture to the masses."

He glanced over at her and she saw something in his gaze that she couldn't define. But it caused a chill to run down her spine.

"That sounds right up your alley."

She realized she'd touched a nerve from his past. The past that had shaped him and driven him to become the man he was today. She knew that he didn't think the masses benefited from Tempest's Closet coming into their small towns. Maybe her article would change his mind.

"I don't know how it'll turn out. I've never written anything other than press releases before."

He signaled to change lanes and then looked over at her. "It'll turn out good like everything else you try."

She flushed at the compliment and at the confidence and pride she saw in his eyes. He pleased her on so many levels that sometimes she woke up afraid that this was all a dream. The fragile bond they'd formed two weeks ago should have made her feel more sure of their relationship but it had only made her realize how vulnerable they were.

"I was thinking about staying in for dinner tonight. Kali's hosting a birthday party for one of her coworkers but I thought a quiet night would be better."

"I'm going to be later at work tonight than I thought. Why don't you go to the party and we'll catch up later?"

He hadn't mentioned that earlier. She didn't want to go to the party by herself. She was slowly coming to realize that socializing wasn't what she really took pleasure in. She'd come to really enjoy the evenings that she spent home with him. Just curled up on the sofa while he worked or watched TV.

"Oh. Okay. I'll go to her party."

"You don't have to go if you don't want to. I thought you might not want to stay home by yourself."

"You're right. What kind of socialite stays in when there's a party?" She tried for a flippancy she didn't feel and knew she'd failed miserably when he glanced over at her.

"What was that tone about?"

"Nothing."

"Tempest…"

What could she say that wasn't going to make her

sound like an idiot and make him tense up on her? She knew better than to confront him with anything to do with Tempest's Closet and her father. Yet it was so much a part of her life—she couldn't ignore her heritage any more than he could.

"I don't have to write the article. I know you don't really agree with everything that Tempest's Closet has done."

He didn't say anything but pulled the car into a parking lot and turned to face her. "I'm not bailing on dinner because of an article you're writing."

"Really?" she asked, doubting him. There was something going on here. Something more than he'd ever admit to. She wondered if it had to do with Michael and whatever the two of them had been discussing when she'd arrived in his office.

He nodded. "I'm proud that you're going to do an article for *Vogue*. I think it'll be a great career transition for you. A way for you to stand on your own and show everyone that there's so much more to Tempest Lambert than a high-society heiress."

The relief she felt was so intense she thought she might cry. What the hell was wrong with her? Her emotions were taking her on a roller coaster ride and she wanted off. She wanted to find a nice safe place in her relationship with Gavin and had the feeling that it would never happen.

"A high-society mistress," she said. That phrase always made her feel a little smarmy. Like she wasn't good enough for Gavin to consider her as anything other than a mistress. She knew it was just a scintillating title that the magazines used to entice readers. But it did tarnish a little of what they had together.

"I've talked to my lawyer about suing the tabloids but he said that would only add fuel to the fire."

"I wish there was some way to make them back off. Should we stop seeing each other?"

"No, baby. Move in with me permanently."

Throughout lunch all he'd been able to think about was what Michael had said. He was going to tear apart Tempest's heritage. *Her legacy.* But it was too late to swerve from that course of action. His entire life would be a lie if he broke the vow he'd made at sixteen.

The vow that someday August Lambert would fall to him. There was no way to stop everything he put in motion. By the end of October when Tempest's Closet held their annual shareholders meeting, Renard Investments would be the majority shareholder and he would demand that August step down as CEO.

And he didn't want to lose Tempest. The only way to keep her was to get her into his house now. To enmesh their lives so tightly together that when the changes happened at Tempest's Closet she would have something else. Something with him.

Oh, hell, she was staring at him like he'd lost his mind. Maybe he could have phrased it better. He should have waited until they were out of the car at least. He was acting like the animal he was beneath his Turnball & Asser designer clothes. The animal that he tried time and again to hide from her.

"Are you sure you want me to move in with you?" she asked. Her fingers were twisted together in her lap. She'd spent a lifetime by herself. Since her mother died she'd been on her own. Would she want to live with him? They were both loners, he thought. Of course with him it was obvious but only someone who'd really gotten to know Tempest like he had would recognize the solitary way she moved through her scores of friends.

"I wouldn't have asked if I wasn't," he said, but he sounded angry. And she was looking at him like he'd lost his mind.

"I'm making a mess of this."

He was known for his cool demeanor and had convinced more than one hesitant investor to go with an investment based solely on his word. He could convince Tempest to do this. He hadn't made himself into the man he was today by vacillating.

"You are. This isn't like you."

But he realized that it was like the man he wanted to be. This was the answer he thought he might have been searching for since that first night he'd made her his.

Reaching across the seat he cupped the back of her head and drew her forward until their lips met. He felt her surprise but her mouth opened under his. He thrust his tongue deep inside her, tasting her completely.

Hell, he really wanted to marry her. To legally make her his but he knew he couldn't do that until he had taken control of Tempest's Closet and that mess was behind them.

Her hands crept around his neck and her fingers slid beneath his collar getting closer to him, touching his skin. He wanted more. But this wasn't the place for seduction.

He pulled back, brushing his mouth over hers because he didn't want to stop kissing her. He never wanted to stop tasting her.

"Say yes," he said.

She stared up at him and in her clear blue eyes he saw all of her hopes and her dreams. And he hoped that he was man enough to live up to them. He was so afraid that he couldn't. Because he knew that he'd been doing the ultimate snow job on her. Convincing her that he was a whole man when inside he was empty. When inside he'd been eaten up by that long ago vow. And only now that she was in his heart did he feel like he was starting to be someone completely whole.

"I'm not an easy person to live with."

"Neither am I."

"My phone rings all the time."

"That's okay. I bring my work home with me every night."

"I can't cook."

"Mrs. Stanton takes care of that."

She was throwing up things that were inconsequential but he sensed there was more to her arguments. "What's this really about?"

"I've never lived with anyone. Not since my mother died."

He hadn't realized that. "You mean as an adult, right?"

"No, even as a child. When mother died, my father kept me at boarding school or summer camps. We'd meet at hotels for different holidays."

This was her legacy, he thought. This was what August Lambert had left her with. Suddenly he felt a hell of a lot better about his plans for Tempest's Closet. A man with priorities that screwed up deserved to have the rug jerked out from under him.

"Those things don't matter to me. We're practically living together every weekend. I think we do okay."

She looked into his eyes searchingly and he wondered what she wanted to see in his gaze. He really hoped she'd find it.

"Are you sure?" she asked. He recognized the hope underlying her words.

"I am very sure. I've never really had much of a home, either, but I want to try to make one with you."

She nibbled on her lower lip and then took a deep breath.

"Yes," she said at last. Her voice was so soft he

was afraid he'd misunderstood but he knew he hadn't.

"Great. I'll call the movers when I get back to my office."

"There's no hurry," she said. "I know you're busy."

"Not too busy for this, Tempest. I'm not too busy for you."

"I never thought you were."

He would do everything to make her feel like an integral part of his life. To make her see that even though he couldn't give up his revenge, he wouldn't give up on her, either.

Eleven

Tempest had been to the Shedd Aquarium more times than she could remember for different functions and events. But tonight felt just a little magical as she entered on Gavin's arm. It could be that this was the first function they'd attended since she'd moved into his house. Or maybe it was just the fact that they'd been together for three months.

Earlier this evening, Gavin had made sweet love to her on his king-sized bed when she'd come out of the shower. Her entire body was still tingling. He glanced down at her and she blushed, thinking of the way she'd begged him to take her.

He raised one eyebrow. "What are you thinking about?"

"Nothing."

"Nothing, hmm, I'm thinking about the way you felt when I—"

She put her hand over his mouth. "Stop it, don't say that out loud."

He waggled his eyebrows, kissing the inside of her hand as he pulled it from his mouth. "Well, I am."

Someone cleared their throat behind them and Tempest glanced over Gavin's shoulder, meeting her father's disapproving gaze.

He wore his tuxedo with panache and ease. He'd always seemed so well put together that she felt she'd never measure up. But with Gavin's arm around her waist…she didn't feel like she was lacking.

She'd found her place in the world after a lifetime of searching. She wished she were alone with Gavin because she'd tell him right now. She'd confess the love that she'd been carrying as a secret in her heart. What good was love if it was kept inside?

She slid her own arm around Gavin's waist and leaned closer to him. He squeezed her hip.

"Good evening, Tempest."

"Hello, Father," she said. Gavin turned so they were both facing August. He looked tired and a little tense but then the retail business was a stressful one. She smiled at her father though she sensed an underlying tension between the two men.

Her mind was a total blank, which didn't surprise her. Her father unnerved her as no other person could. She always felt like she was thirteen years old and trapped between being a child and an adult. She felt awkward and gawky.

"Father, you know Gavin Renard, right?"

Her father nodded and held out his hand.

Gavin shook it. "Evening, August."

An awkward silence fell among the three of them. Tempest saw Kali over her father's shoulder trying to get away from the people she was with and come to the rescue.

"Doesn't the aquarium look nice tonight?" she said, desperate to overcome the awkwardness of this conversation.

Gavin glanced down at her. She hoped he realized that this wasn't the place for the conversation he wanted to have with her father.

"Yes, it does. But then it is always spectacular."

"Yes it is. Renard, will you excuse us? I'd like to speak to my daughter in private."

Gavin excused himself and her father led the way to one of the small quiet alcoves that had been set with cocktail tables.

Her apprehension about dealing with her father was stronger than ever tonight. There was something almost solemn about him and she just couldn't put her finger on what was wrong.

"What did you want to talk to me about?"

"About your being Gavin's mistress."

She wrapped an arm around her waist. Was he concerned for her? She cautioned herself not to read too much into his attention. The last time she had…well she'd been more than disappointed. But this was the first time since her mother died that he'd engaged her in a private conversation that had nothing to do with Tempest's Closet.

"I'm not really his mistress. The gossip columnists just keep saying that. But we are actually living together now. I think he might be the one." She hoped her father had gotten beyond believing what he read about her in magazines and newspapers.

"The one what?" August asked.

"The one I marry."

"I doubt that."

"Why?" she asked. Her father didn't know Gavin like she did.

"He's after Tempest's Closet."

"Dad, that's business. Gavin would never let that affect his relationship with me."

"What makes you so sure?"

She didn't know. She could say that it was her gut but she knew her father wouldn't accept that answer.

"I just am."

"Don't set yourself up for disappointment, Tempest. I'd like to think I raised you to be pragmatic if nothing else."

He turned to walk away and she almost let him go. "Father?"

"Yes?"

"You didn't raise me. Boarding schools and nannies did," she said, brushing past him. "And you don't know the man Gavin is away from the business world. He'd never hurt me the way you have."

He stopped her with a hand on her arm. "He already has. He's taking over Tempest's Closet and forcing all the family out. That includes you."

"What are you talking about?"

"Maybe you don't know your man as well as you think you do," he said.

"Just tell me what's going on," she said.

"Maybe we should let Renard do that. Tell her, Gavin."

Gavin stepped out of the shadows, coming to stand next to her and her father. She looked up into his eyes willing him to laugh and make light of her father's comments but he was too somber. There was more than a kernel of truth in her father's words. She shouldn't have been shocked by that. Her father never joked around when it came to business.

Gavin hated the way Tempest stood with her arm wrapped around her waist. His instincts had said letting her go off with her father had been a bad idea. But he wasn't about to shelter her from the truth.

"Tell me what exactly?"

"I'm not sure," Gavin said. He didn't know how much information August already knew.

"Something about your buying up shares in Tempest's Closet and forcing the family out."

August's information was complete. Gavin wondered if he had a leak in his own organization or if the boys at Tempest's Closet had finally gotten smart.

"I didn't buy up the shares; Renard Investments did on behalf of a consortium of investors. I've only just spoken with our investors this afternoon and we haven't made any decisions on what we will be doing with Tempest's Closet at this point."

Tempest was watching him with those wide blue eyes of hers and he had this sinking feeling that living with him wasn't going to be insulation enough from the shock brought in by his ruthless business maneuverings. That somehow she was going to slip through his fingers tonight.

"You are Renard Investments. Whatever you recommend to those investors they will do."

"That's true."

"Put my father's mind at ease, Gavin. Tell him you're not going to tear the company he built apart."

He stared at her and knew that this was going to be the moment when he lost her. Because he couldn't do what she was asking him. He wasn't going to put August Lambert's mind at ease.

He wanted the older man to spend as many sleepless nights as his father had. He wanted the older man to be forced to come begging to him for his job. And then he wanted—oh, hell, he craved—the opportunity to tell him no.

"This really isn't the place to discuss business. Call my secretary in the morning, August, and I'll try to squeeze you in."

"I'm not going to come to your office."

"That's your decision. But I think we both know that you are over-extended and I know I hold all the cards."

"And my daughter," August said.

Gavin nodded. He would have preferred to do this away from Tempest. To keep her out of the seedier side of what he did. The fact was hostile take-overs were never pretty. They were down and dirty fighting. The kind he was best at.

And she'd always seen him as something more than he was. Maybe this was for the best. Let her see the man he really was so that she'd know exactly what he had to offer her.

Except with Tempest he was a different man.

"I'm with him because I want to be. Our relationship has nothing to do with Tempest's Closet," she said.

"I'm not so sure about that. This is a man who has the money and power to control the media and yet he still allows them to refer to you as his mistress. He's not the one for you, Tempest."

She glanced at him and he saw the doubt in her eyes. But he wasn't about to defend himself against these ridiculous accusations. Tempest herself asked him not to bother with the stories the scandal rags had been running.

"I asked him to leave the media alone. These kind of stories blow over."

"You always were good at believing whatever lies you told yourself."

She visibly recoiled from her father and Gavin reached out, pulling her to his side and tucking her up against him. "You direct your anger toward me, Lambert. Tempest has nothing to do with this business between us."

"She has everything to do with it. You placed her squarely between us."

"Even I can't control who I fall for."

"Are you saying you care for her?"

Gavin wasn't sure he wanted to do this now. Do this here. But not confirming his feelings for her wasn't going to help anyone.

He glanced down at Tempest. Leaning close he whispered into her ear. "Yes."

She wrapped one arm around his waist, holding him tightly to her. "Me, too."

He wanted to pick her up and carry her away from this place. Away from the crowds filling the aquarium and away from the man who was watching them.

"If he really loves you, then he won't destroy the only legacy I have to give you."

"Of course, he isn't going to destroy it," she said. "That's not your intent is it, Gavin?"

Destroying Tempest's Closet had been his goal for far too long. There was no way he could give it up even for Tempest. Her legacy wasn't a chain of retail stores. Her legacy was the writing she'd be doing. Sharing her past with readers and talking about a unique point in fashion history that her father established.

"I'm not at liberty to discuss this right now. We can talk either in my office tomorrow, Lambert, or at the stockholders' meeting in two weeks."

August gave him a tight smug smile. "That's exactly what I thought. You'll never let my company stay as it is."

"It is a failing business," Gavin said.

"It's an institution like Macy's. You can't close us down."

"I'm not sure what course of action we will take. And I'm not discussing it further tonight."

"Why not? Afraid Tempest will see the real man she's involved with?"

"She already knows exactly who I am."

"Does she?"

"Yes."

"Then tell her the truth of what you plan to do with Tempest's Closet."

"Okay then, I will. I'm going to sell it off piece by piece. Are you satisfied, August?"

Tempest watched her father walk away and then she pushed out of Gavin's arms. Surely he wasn't really going to ruin a company that employed so many people. Surely his hatred of her father and Tempest's Closet didn't go that far.

"Did you mean that?"

"Yes."

The music started in the other room as the party got into full swing. But she felt less like partying than she ever had before. She didn't know how to reach Gavin. She knew that her father represented something dark and dangerous from his past. Something that had shaped him.

But the man she'd fallen in love with wasn't the kind of man who'd take away the livelihood of so many.

"You'll be little better than he is if you do this."

"It's not about him or you. Don't worry about it, Tempest."

"I'm not worrying. I just think that you haven't thought this through."

"I assure you I've thought it through. I've been running a successful company for more than a decade. I think I know what I'm doing."

"You're wrong."

"Wrong?"

"Yes, you're too emotional about my father—"

"Stop right there. I'm not emotional about this. Taking over Tempest's Closet is just another day at the office to me."

Except it wasn't and she knew it. Tempest's Closet represented something to him that no other company could. She took his hand in hers.

"Think of the families that will be put out of work if you do this. Families that have been making a good living—"

"Tempest I care for you, but I can't and won't change my mind on this."

She pulled back. "I'm not trying to manipulate you."

"Good because you can't."

She dropped his hand. "You're life will be empty, Gavin if you do this."

"Are you threatening me?" he asked.

She remembered the last time he'd said those words to her. And they'd come out of that moment stronger in their commitment to each other. She knew she just had to find the right words to say.

Find the thing that would relax him and once he got some distance from the confrontation with her father maybe he'd calm down and be able to talk to her rationally.

"I asked you a question, Tempest."

"Don't speak to me like that," she said. "You know I'm not threatening you."

"Really?"

"Really."

"The consortium has already agreed to tear the company apart and sell it off. It's the only way to make a profit. Are you still going to stay with me?"

"You're acting like a jerk."

"No, I'm acting like a man whose woman is trying to get him to make a business decision that makes no sense."

"I'm trying to get you to see that there's no prospect for a man who can only destroy things. For a man who doesn't see that only by building things and creating new opportunities can there be a real future."

"A real future with you?"

"With anyone, Gavin. You have to let go of the past."

"Would you be so concerned if my past involved any company other than Tempest's Closet?"

She stared at him for a long moment and realized that she had fooled herself into thinking that he really wasn't the man the media made him out to be. That he wasn't the man *Forbes* had called a 'cold-blooded profit maker.' Because the stories written about her were never true.

"The sad thing is that you have to ask me that."

"Sad because it's true. You know you like the money you make from Tempest's Closet. You haven't had a job for the entire time we've been together."

"I don't have to work because my mother left me a trust that pays me an annuity. I don't live off the profits I make from Tempest's Closet. They are re-invested in the company."

"Whatever you say."

"I don't have to explain myself to you."

"Neither do I."

There was a finality to his words that made her realize he'd anticipated this sort of ending for them. And it was an ending. She saw it in his eyes and in his stance.

"I wasn't asking for an explanation," she said, pushing a tendril of hair back behind her ear and realizing her hand was shaking.

"What were you asking for?"

She had no idea. This argument had gotten totally out of her control. To be honest she no longer was angry at him. Instead she was sad because she couldn't see a way around this situation. Couldn't find a way that she and Gavin could have something lasting. Ever. It wasn't about Tempest's Closet or the small town that he'd grown up in.

She had a moment of true clarity seeing Gavin as she'd never seen him before. He was an emotionally damaged man focused only on business, one who'd taught himself to hide away from the world.

She recognized that because she did it herself. She hid behind fashion and the paparazzi. But she'd always craved a man like him. A place like his arms where she could curl up and forget the outside world existed.

"I was asking for you to let go of the anger and bitterness that's controlled your life so long and take a chance on love."

"I'm not bitter," he said.

She just shook her head and walked away. Not knowing what else to say to him.

Twelve

Tempest left the Shedd Aquarium and caught a cab out front. But she had no idea where to go. She couldn't go back to Gavin's place and she had no interest in going to her empty condo. She wanted to find a quiet place where she could just break down and cry.

She felt tears stinging her eyes but she forced them back. Actually she didn't want to cry. She wanted to find a nice numb place where she couldn't feel.

What was it about her that she couldn't see the men in the life for what they were?

The cabbie was looking at her, waiting for an address, and finally she sighed. She had no idea where to go. She thought Kali would take her in but that would be humiliating beyond measure.

How could she have been so wrong about Gavin? Her cell phone rang and she glanced at the caller ID display before answering the call. *Gavin.*

"Where are you going?" he asked.

"I don't know," she said. She hated the way her voice sounded thready and weak. She didn't want him to realize how deep his rejection had cut her. As if there were any way she could hide that. Gavin had always seen straight through the masks she wore to fool others.

"I'll crash at Michael's tonight. Go back to my place."

There was no way she was going back to his place. Not even to get her things. She didn't want to remember the illusions she'd bought into while she'd been there.

She didn't want to remember what it had been like to be happy for those few short months. It was almost the way she'd felt about her father's house on Lake Shore Drive. That big mansion that she'd lived in when her mother had been alive but had rarely set foot in after her death.

"Thanks but I don't think I'll do that. I can find a friend to stay with."

That weird sound of silence buzzed on the open line and she bit her lower lip hoping…what? That he'd somehow say he was an idiot and that he was going to give up making a huge profit just to make her happy.

She sighed, missing him more than she should, considering he'd just told her taking revenge on her father mattered more than she did. But her heart didn't care about Gavin's revenge. All her heart cared about was that she'd be sleeping alone in a big bed without him by her side. She'd be waking and reading the newspaper by herself. Her life would go back to its busy but empty schedule.

"Goodbye, Gavin."

"Tempest?" There was a note of pleading in his voice that made her hope. Was he going to alter his plans for Tempest's Closet?

"Yes."

"If I could change…"

"You can," she said, believing it with all her heart.

"But not on this. In the future I can be a different man, maybe start building things instead of buying them and then selling them off piece by piece."

She knew that it would be too late. Too late for them because, whether Gavin knew it or not, putting all those families who relied on Tempest's Closet for their livelihood out of work was going to affect him.

"I hope you do change," she said, softly.

"But it's too late for you. Is that what you are saying?"

She wished she had a different answer but she didn't. "Yes."

"I thought you cared for me."

"I do. More than you'll ever know but I can't keep shifting who I am to please you."

"I've never asked you to do that."

"You did tonight when you said that Tempest's Closet wasn't part of my legacy."

"This really is over?"

It broke her heart to say it but they both knew it was true. "Yes."

"Take care, then."

He disconnected the call and she hugged her phone to her chest. The cabbie was still looking at her and she figured she was making a fool of herself. "The Ritz-Carlton at Water Tower Place."

Her family had long kept a suite at the hotel. She'd crash there tonight and in the morning make some solid plans. One thing was—she needed to get a job, start working to get her mind off things. The article for *Vogue* was something, but not enough.

The sites of the city she'd always called home flashed by the window as the driver wove through traffic. She realized she was going to have to leave Chicago. Not just temporarily, but forever. She needed to get as far away from the men in her life and the humiliation she felt at having tried to make them love her. To make herself more important than their business machinations. More important than their workaholic schedules. More important than their game of one-upmanship. She'd lost but good and it was time to leave.

She wished the decision was an easy one, but inside she felt a tearing deep in her heart and she knew it was going to be a long time before she forgot Gavin Renard.

It started to rain as the cab pulled to a stop in front of the hotel. The doorman opened the cab for her and she stepped out, forcing a smile on her face. Time to start pretending she was Tempest Lambert, happy-go-lucky heiress.

The heiress who didn't care that the world knew her business. She made sure that she lingered in the lobby, chatting with a couple she knew from her childhood. She was careful to keep the smile and lighthearted banter foremost until the door to her 30th floor suite closed behind her and she sank to the floor leaning back against the wood door.

Gavin went to the table he'd reserved for the event and sat down. But he was scarcely aware of anything going on around him. He knew he should be making plans. Now that August knew he had enough shares to force him out there was a chance the other man would try to manipulate the stock somehow.

But he couldn't focus on that just now. Where was Tempest going? Why had he let her leave like that?

He just wasn't willing to give into any kind of ultimatum. It didn't matter that she hadn't really been telling him he had to choose between her or Tempest's Closet. He knew in his heart he couldn't have both.

And he'd only known Tempest for a few months. He'd been focused on Tempest's Closet since he was sixteen years old.

"Where's Tempest?" Michael asked as he seated Melinda and then took his seat.

Gavin hoped that he'd never have to answer that question again. But since it was Michael he knew he couldn't ignore it. In fact, considering that they'd become friends he was probably going to have to endure more than one question. "Gone."

"What? Is she okay? Melinda had a sinus headache earlier."

"Tempest's health is fine. August is here."

"Did he say something to her?" Michael asked. "You know he's the most arrogant men I've ever met. When I called him with your offer he said he'd rather rot in hell than do business with us."

Because of Tempest he had asked Michael to put together a package for August that would give the other man a figurehead position with no power but at least would let him hold on to his pride. And more importantly, to ease the shock and pain for Tempest. But that cold bastard had found another way to twist the knife in.

"He knows we have purchased all those shares that were available and somehow he knows that we're behind Hugh Stephen's loan, too. I think we need to go back to the office and look for a leak."

"Tonight?" Melinda asked.

"Yes," he said. Yes, definitely tonight. He needed to get to work. Work had been his salvation once and it would be again.

"Gav, are you sure about this? Shouldn't you go after Tempest instead?"

Michael was right—and it really pissed him off.

He wasn't going after her. Not now. He'd have to beg her to come back and he wasn't into begging.

"When have I ever asked you for advice?" Hell, he hated asking for anything.

"Never, but maybe you should start."

He admired Michael more than any other man he'd ever met but that didn't mean he was going to listen to him when it came to Tempest. Michael couldn't begin to understand that complex woman. Hell, half the time he didn't.

"You're not exactly a great example of success when it comes to relationships," Gavin said.

"I asked Melinda to marry me," Michael said, turning to her and drawing her into his arms.

A future. This is what Gavin should be planning instead of how to make August squirm. This is what he should be focused on instead of a quest for vengeance that would never bring him peace. "Wow, that's big. Why didn't you mention it to me?"

Michael ducked his head, rubbing one hand over his chest. "I wanted to make sure she said yes first."

"Congratulations, bro. I'm happy for you. Welcome to the family, Melinda."

Michael reached across the table, his hand falling on Gavin's shoulder. "You could be happy, too."

Not anymore. Not now that he'd seen the way Tempest had so easily believed the worst in him. Granted he hadn't tried that hard to convince her otherwise. Not that her opinion of him was what stopped him from going back to her. What really kept him in his seat was the pain he'd seen in those glittery blue eyes of hers.

Beyond the anger had been the kind of soul-deep pain that he wasn't sure he had the right to ask her to forgive him for causing. And the root cause remained, because he sure as hell wasn't backing down from August. The one tentative olive branch he'd offered had been rebuffed, and to be honest, he wasn't interested in trying that hard to win over her old man.

"You should get out of here and take Melinda some place nice to celebrate."

"I'm going to. We're just dropping in for a few minutes. I'm taking tomorrow off."

"Enjoy yourself."

His brother hesitated before walking away and Gavin forced a smile to reassure him. He was happier for Michael than he could express. The table filled up with business associates until there was only one empty spot left. The chair that should have been Tempest's.

He talked with those around him, functioned as close to normal as he could. He had the feeling that this was the life he'd made for himself. That there'd always be that vacant chair in his mind that should be filled with her.

Ah, hell, he was getting maudlin. Was he really letting her go? Was there really no way to keep her?

He left as soon as the dinner was served. Instead of driving home he cruised the city finding himself on Lake Shore Drive. He slowed at the gated mansion where August Lambert lived and glanced up there.

For Tempest's sake he knew he should at least make an effort to smooth things over with her father. He wasn't going to give in to her old man. But he was a shrewd negotiator willing to do whatever it took. And he wasn't going to leave the Lake Shore Lambert mansion until he and August had hammered out a deal that gave him what he wanted—a way back into Tempest's heart.

Revenge wasn't as sweet as he'd always hoped it would be. And seeing Michael get everything that Gavin had secretly dreamed of having with Tempest had twisted the sword of her leaving in his gut a little bit.

Sitting in his luxury car and watching August's house he realized that maybe it was time that he did become a better man.

He pulled up to the gate and rang the bell. He didn't know if August had left the Shedd yet or not. But Gavin could wait. He would wait as long as he had to and use the time to figure out a way to make the situation with Tempest's Closet right. August was going to agree to his terms because if he didn't the old man would really end up with nothing. And if he accepted Gavin's deal to remain part of the company then he'd still have not only a job to go to each day but also a chance at a relationship with the daughter he'd never had time for.

Then once Gavin was finished with August, he

was going after Tempest. Because even a few hours without her in his life was too long.

The bed was too big and the halls too quiet. After nearly a week at the Ritz she realized that her old habits were back. She was sleeping maybe two hours a night. No matter how she tried she couldn't get comfortable in her sleep, she kept rolling over and searching for Gavin.

She tossed and turned in the king-sized bed one more time before finally getting up. Wrapping herself in a robe she went to the windows and glanced down at the streets. Unlike Manhattan that was busy 24/7, Chicago did sleep in the wee hours of the night.

She pushed her hair to one side and wished that she could calm the voices in her head. The ones that warned her that maybe she'd overreacted and that she should go back and try one more time to make Gavin see reason.

She wandered around the room filled with a feeling of nothing, of that emptiness that made her want to do something crazy. Finally it was a six o'clock and she changed into her workout clothes and went down to the gym.

While she was running on the treadmill, everything coalesced. She didn't need to leave Chicago, she needed to find her place here.

She realized no matter how hard she ran or how far she moved away, the past would always be with her.

The past defined who she was today in a way that she'd never realized before. Asking Gavin to give up his revenge was like asking him to stop breathing. She'd heard his sparse tales of the past. Understood that her father and Tempest's Closet had changed the course of his life—and given him something to drive toward.

She left the gym, grabbed a bottle of water and headed for the elevator. She stepped into the car. After her shower she was going to make some real plans for the day.

"Hold the door."

She put her hand out between the doors to keep it from closing. She never could figure out which icon button meant door-open.

Gavin stepped into the car. He had on jeans and a rumpled Harvard T-shirt. His hair was mussed and he had stubble on his jaw. He looked tired but so good to her that she wanted to jump in his arms. She'd missed him more than she'd wanted to.

"What are you doing here?" she asked. Their last conversation had felt so final that she'd never expected to see or hear from him again. And clearly dressed the way he was, he wasn't here for a meeting.

"Looking for you."

"How did you find me?" she asked. The only people who knew she was here were the hotel staff and Kali. Kali had come over the first night she'd arrived.

"Kali."

"I can't believe she told you where I am." Kali had been as angry at Gavin as Tempest had been.

"Um…she didn't. I had to go to Michael and ask him for Melinda's help to call Kali."

"What?"

"Can we talk about this in your room?"

"Sure."

She couldn't believe he was here. Or that Kali had given up her location.

She led the way down the hall to her room with Gavin following closely behind her. He hadn't said another word on the ride.

She opened the door and stepped inside, seeing the mess she'd made of the room. The open box of chocolates on the table, the empty tea mug and the robe she'd left lying over the back of the couch.

She walked to the window and leaned against the wall next to it. The city was just coming awake.

"Okay, so explain to me what you're doing here."

"I wanted…I mean you were…ah, hell, Tempest. I don't know what to say."

She wrapped an arm around her waist and stared at him. He'd never really been too vocal about what he felt. But the fact that he was here meant something. But she was afraid to speculate on what it meant. Afraid to hope that he was here because he wanted a future with her.

"Start at the beginning. You went to Michael?"

"Kali wouldn't take any of my calls, well, except for one."

"And you asked her where I was?"

"I never got the chance. You should know that you have a really good friend in her."

"I do know it. I also know she has a bad temper."

"So I found out," he said.

She wanted to smile at the way he said it. "After that you went to Michael?"

"No. I called every hotel in the city but no one would give me any information about you. I checked the airlines and you weren't listed on any flights out. Same with trains so I had a pretty good hunch you were still in the city."

"Why did you do all that?" she asked, no longer caring how he found her.

"Because I need you."

"You need me?"

"You were right when you said that I couldn't keep living my life the way I always had. I treat everything like its temporary and try to insulate myself from disappointment. But when you left…there was no insulation."

"I never meant to hurt you."

"I know. I didn't mean to hurt you, either, but I did."

He crossed the room to her, pulling her away from the wall and into his arms. And though she wasn't sure she should, she wrapped her arms around his waist. He crushed her to his chest and she held him back just as fiercely.

Cupping her face in his hands, he tipped her head

backward. "I don't want a life without you. I like the man I am when you're around me."

Her heart sped up at his words and she saw real affection and caring in his eyes. "Oh, Gavin, what are you saying?"

"I'm saying I love you and I want you to marry me."

He kissed her then before she could say a word in response. His tongue thrusting past the barrier of her teeth and tongue. His hands sweeping down her back and holding her molded to the front of his body.

When he lifted his head, she started to speak but he rubbed his thumb over her lower lip. "I should have said this first. Your father and I are working out a plan for Tempest's Closet—it's not the role he's used to and he'll have to work for our new CEO but I think he's considering it. The consortium has agreed to allow Michael to step in as CEO for a year. Michael has a solid plan to get Tempest's Closet back on track."

"Dad agreed to that?"

"He didn't really have a choice. It was take the deal or walk away with nothing."

She stared up into his gray eyes finally believing that he really did love her.

"I love you, Gavin."

"And you'll marry me?"

"Yes."

He kissed her hard and carried her into the bedroom. Making love to her as if it had been years

since they'd been together instead of just an incredibly long week. Knowing they had both found
the home they'd been searching for.

Epilogue

Her father's chauffeur-driven Mercedes arrived promptly at 7:35 p.m. Tempest nervously smoothed her hands down the simple lines of her white satin wedding dress. The last nine months had flown by and her new life was everything she'd always dreamed it would be.

Her father climbed out of the back of the car while Marcus, his driver, stood holding the door open.

Tempest stood at the top of the steps looking down at her father. Their relationship was still a little awkward but he'd been making an effort to get to know her and she was getting to know him, as well. He said that Gavin's take-over had forced him to realize there was more to life than Tempest's Closet.

So here she was trying not to smile too brightly but when her father glanced up at her, she couldn't help it.

"You're so beautiful, Tempest. You look just like your mother."

"Thank you, Father," she said around the lump in her throat, her nerves melting away at the compliment. This was her night. The night when she and Gavin were going to be married at her father's estate.

The tabloids had stopped referring to her as a high-society anything.

The drive to the Lake Shore mansion was quick. There was a silence between her and her father that wasn't exactly comfortable but it wasn't as strained as it would have been in the past. "Thanks for agreeing to let us have the wedding here."

"Your mother would have wanted you to be married in her gardens."

"She did love her garden," Tempest said.

"She also loved you, Tempest. Every night before she went to sleep she'd remind me how lucky we were to have you."

Tears burned the back of her eyes. She had so few memories of her mother, and her father had never spoken of her before. This small nugget about her mom was like a precious gift.

She blinked rapidly, stopping the tears that threatened.

"Are you sure about marrying Renard?"

"Yes," she said. She wasn't nervous about marrying Gavin.

Flashbulbs exploded as they passed a knot of paparazzi who were clustered around the gated drive of her father's mansion. She and Gavin had agreed to letting *Vogue* magazine—and only *Vogue*—do a profile on their wedding. After all, she had now made a full-time job of writing for them about the fashion industry from the inside.

Her father nodded once as they came to a stop in the drive. Marcus opened the door to the car, and her father came around and took her hand, escorting her through the house and into the back yard.

There were close to a hundred people assembled there. She glanced at the sea of faces not really seeing them. Her father walked down the aisle ahead of her and took a seat up front. She'd decided against asking him to give her away since he'd never really had her. Instead she glanced to the right and saw Gavin waiting for her.

"You are gorgeous," he said, coming to her side and kissing her passionately on the lips.

"So are you," she said, feeling the love he felt for her flow through her. Feeling surrounded by the love she felt for him.

"Even though I'm not model material?" he asked, making her smile.

"Even though."

He dropped another quick kiss on her lips.

"Can't you wait for the honeymoon to do that?" Michael asked coming up behind them.

"Mind your own business, bro."

"I guess I finally can now that Tempest is in your life."

Michael winked at her. "He needs a lot of advice, Tempest. Are you sure you want to take him on?"

"Very sure," she said.

"You messed up her lipstick," Kali said, stepping up beside Tempest. "Give me a minute to fix it then we can get this wedding started."

Kali fixed Tempest's lipstick and then hugged her. Leaning close to her to whisper, "I'm so happy for you."

The wedding fanfare started and Kali and Michael walked up the aisle in front of Tempest and Gavin. They had decided on a simple wedding with only Kali and Michael as their attendants.

As the Wedding March began to play, Tempest glanced up at Gavin and knew he'd given her the kind of happiness she'd always thought she could never find. She couldn't wait for the ceremony to be over so that they would be legally bound, though in her heart she knew nothing would ever take him from her side. They worked hard to build a future they'd both be proud of. And Gavin had been talking about children and building a dynasty together. She thought about what her father had said to her long ago about choices—and realized she'd made the right one when she'd approached Gavin.

* * * * *

Every Life Has More
Than One Chapter™

Award-winning author Stevi Mittman delivers
another hysterical mystery, featuring Teddi
Bayer, an irrepressible heroine, and her to-die-
for hero, Detective Drew Scoones. After all, life
on Long Island can be murder!

*Turn the page for a sneak peek
at the warm and funny fourth book,
WHOSE NUMBER IS UP, ANYWAY?,
in the Teddi Bayer series,
by STEVI MITTMAN.
On sale August 7*

CHAPTER 1

"Before redecorating a room, I always advise my clients to empty it of everything but one chair. Then I suggest they move that chair from place to place, sitting in it, until the placement feels right. Trust your instincts when deciding on furniture placement. Your room should "feel right."

—TipsFromTeddi.com

Gut feelings. You know, that gnawing in the pit of your stomach that warns you that you are about to do the absolute stupidest thing you could do? Something that will ruin life as you know it?

I've got one now, standing at the butcher counter in King Kullen, the grocery store in the same strip mall as L.I. Lanes, the bowling alley cum billiard parlor I'm in the process of redecorating for its "Grand Opening."

I realize being in the wrong supermarket probably doesn't sound exactly dire to you, but you aren't the one buying your father a brisket at a store your mother will somehow know isn't Waldbaum's.

And then, June Bayer isn't your mother.

The woman behind the counter has agreed to go into the freezer to find a brisket for me, since there aren't any in the case. There are packages of pork tenderloin, piles of spare ribs and rolls of sausage, but no briskets.

Warning Number Two, right? I should be so out of here.

But no, I'm still in the same spot when she comes back out, brisketless, her face ashen. She opens her mouth as if she is going to scream, but only a gurgle comes out.

And then she pinballs out from behind the counter, knocking bottles of Peter Luger Steak Sauce to the floor on her way, now hitting the tower of cans at the end of the prepared foods aisle and sending them sprawling, now making her way down the aisle, careening from side to side as she goes.

Finally, from a distance, I hear her shout, "He's deeeeeeaaaad! Joey's deeeeeaaaad."

My first thought is *You should always trust your gut.*

My second thought is that now, somehow, my mother will know I was in King Kullen. For weeks I will have to hear "What did you expect?" as though whenever you go to King Kullen someone turns up dead. And if the detective investigating the case turns out to be Detective Drew Scoones…well, I'll never hear the end of that from her, either.

She still suspects I murdered the guy who was

found dead on my doorstep last Halloween just to get Drew back into my life.

Several people head for the butcher's freezer and I position myself to block them. If there's one thing I've learned from finding people dead—and the guy on my doorstep wasn't the first one—it's that the police get very testy when you mess with their murder scenes.

"You can't go in there until the police get here," I say, stationing myself at the end of the butcher's counter and in front of the Employees Only door, acting as if I'm some sort of authority. "You'll contaminate the evidence if it turns out to be murder."

Shouts and chaos. You'd think I'd know better than to throw the word *murder* around. Cell phones are flipping open and tongues are wagging.

I amend my statement quickly. "Which, of course, it probably isn't. Murder, I mean. People die all the time, and it's not always in hospitals or their own beds, or…" I babble when I'm nervous, and the idea of someone dead on the other side of the freezer door makes me very nervous.

So does the idea of seeing Drew Scoones again. Drew and I have this on-again, off-again sort of thing…that I kind of turned off.

Who knew he'd take it so personally when he tried to get serious and I responded by saying we could talk about *us* tomorrow—and then caught a plane to my parents' condo in Boca the next day? In July. In the middle of a job.

For some crazy reason, he took that to mean that I was avoiding him and the subject of *us*.

That was three months ago. I haven't seen him since.

The manager, who identifies himself and points to his nameplate in case I don't believe him, says he has to go into *his cooler.* "Maybe Joey's not dead," he says. "Maybe he can be saved, and you're letting him die in there. Did you ever think of that?".

In fact, I hadn't. But I had thought that the murderer might try to go back in to make sure his tracks were covered, so I say that I will go in and check.

Which means that the manager and I couple up and go in together while everyone pushes against the doorway to peer in, erasing any chance of finding clean prints on that Employee Only door.

I expect to find carcasses of dead animals hanging from hooks, and maybe Joey hanging from one, too. I think it's going to be very creepy and I steel myself, only to find a rather benign series of shelves with large slabs of meat laid out carefully on them, along with boxes and boxes marked simply Chicken.

Nothing scary here, unless you count the body of a middle-aged man with graying hair sprawled faceup on the floor. His eyes are wide open and un-blinking. His shirt is stiff. His pants are stiff. His body is stiff. And his expression, you should forgive the pun—is frozen. Bill-the-manager crosses himself and stands mute while I pronounce the guy dead in a sort of *happy now?* tone.

"We should not be in here," I say, and he nods his head emphatically and helps me push people out of the doorway just in time to hear the police sirens and see the cop cars pull up outside the big store windows.

Bobbie Lyons, my partner in Teddi Bayer Interior Designs (and also my neighbor, my best friend and my private fashion police), and Mark, our carpenter (and my dogsitter, confidant, and ego booster), rush in from next door. They beat the cops by a half step and shout out my name. People point in my direction.

After all the publicity that followed the unfortunate incident during which I shot my ex-husband, Rio Gallo, and then the subsequent murder of my first client—which I solved, I might add—it seems like the whole world, or at least all of Long Island, knows who I am.

Mark asks if I'm all right. (Did I remember to mention that the man is drop-dead-gorgeous-but-a-decade-too-young-for-me-yet-too-old-for-my-daughter-thank-god?) I don't get a chance to answer him because the police are quickly closing in on the store manager and me.

"The woman—" I begin telling the police. Then I have to pause for the manager to fill in her name, which he does: *Fran.*

I continue. "Right. Fran. Fran went into the

freezer to get a brisket. A moment later she came out and screamed that Joey was dead. So I'd say she was the one who discovered the body."

"And you are…?" the cop asks me. It comes out a bit like who do I *think* I am, rather than who am I really?

"An innocent bystander," Bobbie, hair perfect, makeup just right, says, carefully placing her body between the cop and me.

"And she was just leaving," Mark adds. They each take one of my arms.

Fran comes into the inner circle surrounding the cops. In case it isn't obvious from the hairnet and bloodstained white apron with Fran embroidered on it, I explain that she was the butcher who was going for the brisket. Mark and Bobbie take that as a signal that I've done my job and they can now get me out of there. They twist around, with me in the middle, as if we're a Rockettes line, until we are facing away from the butcher counter. They've managed to propel me a few steps toward the exit when disaster—in the form of a Mazda RX7 pulling up at the loading curb—strikes.

Mark's grip on my arm tightens like a vise. "Too late," he says.

Bobbie's expletive is unprintable. "Maybe there's a back door," she suggests, but Mark is right. It's too late.

I've laid my eyes on Detective Scoones. And while my gut is trying to warn me that my heart shouldn't go there, regions farther south are melting at just the sight of him.

"Walk," Bobbie orders me.

And I try to. Really.

Walk, I tell my feet. *Just put one foot in front of the other.*

I can do this because I know, in my heart of hearts, that if Drew Scoones was still interested in me, he'd have gotten in touch with me after I returned from Boca. And he didn't.

Since he's a detective, Drew doesn't have to wear one of those dark blue Nassau County Police uniforms. Instead, he's got on jeans, a tight-fitting T-shirt and a tweedy sports jacket. If you think that sounds good, you should see him. Chiseled features, cleft chin, brown hair that's naturally a little sandy in the front, a smile that…well, that doesn't matter. He isn't smiling now.

He walks up to me, tucks his sunglasses into his breast pocket and looks me over from head to toe.

"Well, if it isn't Miss Cut and Run," he says. "Aren't you supposed to be somewhere in Florida or something?" He looks at Mark accusingly, as if he was covering for me when he told Drew I was gone.

"Detective Scoones?" one of the uniforms says. "The stiff's in the cooler and the woman who found him is over there." He jerks his head in Fran's direction.

Drew continues to stare at me.

You know how when you were young, your mother always told you to wear clean underwear in case you were in an accident? And how, a little farther on, she told you not to go out in hair rollers because you never knew who you might see—or who might see you? And how now your best friend says she wouldn't be caught dead without makeup and suggests you shouldn't either?

Okay, today, *finally,* in my overalls and Converse sneakers, I get it.

I brush my hair out of my eyes. "Well, I'm back," I say. As if he hasn't known my exact whereabouts. The man is a detective, for heaven's sake. "Been back awhile."

Bobbie has watched the exchange and apparently decided she's given Drew all the time he deserves. "And we've got work to do, so…" she says, grabbing my arm and giving Drew a little two-fingered wave goodbye.

As I back up a foot or two, the store manager sees his chance and places himself in front of Drew, trying to get his attention. Maybe what makes Drew such a good detective is his ability to focus.

Only what he's focusing on is me.

"Phone broken? Carrier pigeon died?" he asks me, taking in Fran, the manager, the meat counter and that Employees Only door, all without taking his eyes off me.

Mark tries to break the spell. "We've got work to do there, you've got work to do here, Scoones,"

Mark says to him, gesturing toward next door. "So it's back to the alley for us."

Drew's lip twitches. "You working the alley now?" he says.

"If you'd like to follow me," Bill-the-manager, clearly exasperated, says to Drew—who doesn't respond. It's as if waiting for my answer is all he has to do.

So, fine. "You knew I was back," I say.

The man has known my whereabouts every hour of the day for as long as I've known him. And my mother's not the only one who won't buy that he "just happened" to answer this particular call. In fact, I'm willing to bet my children's lunch money that he's taken every call within ten miles of my home since the day I got back.

And now he's gotten lucky.

"*You* could have called *me*," I say.

"You're the one who said *tomorrow* for our talk and then flew the coop, chickie," he says. "I figured the ball was in your court."

"Detective?" the uniform says. "There's something you ought to see in here."

Drew gives me a look that amounts to *in or out?*

He could be talking about the investigation, or about our relationship.

Bobbie tries to steer me away. Mark's fists are balled. Drew waits me out, knowing I won't be able to resist what might be a murder investigation.

Finally he turns and heads for the cooler.

And, like a puppy dog, I follow.

Bobbie grabs the back of my shirt and pulls me to a halt.

"I'm just going to show him something," I say, yanking away.

"Yeah," Bobbie says, pointedly looking at the buttons on my blouse. The two at breast level have popped. "That's what I'm afraid of."

HARLEQUIN®

Mediterranean
NIGHTS™

*Glamour, elegance, mystery and revenge
aboard the high seas...*

Coming in August 2007...

THE TYCOON'S
SON

*by
award-winning author*
Cindy Kirk

Businessman Theo Catomeris's long-estranged
father is determined to reconnect with his son, so
he hires Trish Melrose to persuade Theo to renew
his contract with Liberty Line. Sailing aboard the
luxurious *Alexandra's Dream* is a rare opportunity for
the single mom to mix business and pleasure. But
an undeniable attraction between Trish and Theo is
distracting her from the task at hand....

HARLEQUIN®

Super Romance®

*Looking for a romantic, emotional
and unforgettable escape?*

*You'll find it this month and every month
with a Harlequin Superromance!*

Rory Gorenzi has a sense of humor and a sense of
honor. She also happens to be good with children.

Seamus Lee, widower and father of four, needs
someone with exactly those traits.

They meet at the Colorado mountain school owned
by Rory's father, where she teaches skiing and
avalanche safety. But Seamus—and his children—
learn more from her than that….

Look for

GOOD WITH CHILDREN

by *Margot Early,*

*available August 2007, and these other
fantastic titles from Harlequin Superromance.*

REQUEST YOUR FREE BOOKS!

2 FREE NOVELS PLUS 2 FREE GIFTS!

Passionate, Powerful, Provocative!

YES! Please send me 2 FREE Silhouette Desire® novels and my 2 FREE gifts. After receiving them, if I don't wish to receive any more books, I can return the shipping statement marked "cancel." If I don't cancel, I will receive 6 brand-new novels every month and be billed just $3.80 per book in the U.S., or $4.47 per book in Canada, plus 25¢ shipping and handling per book and applicable taxes, if any*. That's a savings of almost 15% off the cover price! I understand that accepting the 2 free books and gifts places me under no obligation to buy anything. I can always return a shipment and cancel at any time. Even if I never buy another book from Silhouette, the two free books and gifts are mine to keep forever.

225 SDN EEXJ 326 SDN EEXU

Name	(PLEASE PRINT)	
Address		Apt.
City	State/Prov.	Zip/Postal Code

Signature (if under 18, a parent or guardian must sign)

Mail to the Silhouette Reader Service™:
IN U.S.A.: P.O. Box 1867, Buffalo, NY 14240-1867
IN CANADA: P.O. Box 609, Fort Erie, Ontario L2A 5X3

Not valid to current Silhouette Desire subscribers.

Want to try two free books from another line?
Call 1-800-873-8635 or visit www.morefreebooks.com.

* Terms and prices subject to change without notice. NY residents add applicable sales tax. Canadian residents will be charged applicable provincial taxes and GST. This offer is limited to one order per household. All orders subject to approval. Credit or debit balances in a customer's account(s) may be offset by any other outstanding balance owed by or to the customer. Please allow 4 to 6 weeks for delivery.

Your Privacy: Silhouette is committed to protecting your privacy. Our Privacy Policy is available online at www.eHarlequin.com or upon request from the Reader Service. From time to time we make our lists of customers available to reputable firms who may have a product or service of interest to you. If you would prefer we not share your name and address, please check here. ☐

SDES07

REASONS FOR REVENGE

A brand-new provocative miniseries by *USA TODAY*
bestselling author **Maureen Child** begins with

SCORNED
BY THE BOSS

Jefferson Lyon is a man used to having his own way.
He runs his shipping empire from California, and
his admin Caitlyn Monroe runs the rest of his world.
When Caitlin decides she's had enough and needs
new scenery, Jefferson devises a plan to get her back.
Jefferson *never* loses, but little does he know that
he's in a competition....

Don't miss any of the other titles from the
REASONS FOR REVENGE trilogy by
USA TODAY bestselling author **Maureen Child.**

SCORNED BY THE BOSS #1816
Available August 2007

SEDUCED BY THE RICH MAN #1820
Available September 2007

CAPTURED BY THE BILLIONAIRE #1826
Available October 2007

Only from Silhouette Desire!

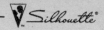

SPECIAL EDITION™

Look for

THE BILLIONAIRE NEXT DOOR

by Jessica Bird

For Wall Street hotshot Sean O'Banyon, going home to south Boston brought back bad memories. But Lizzie Bond, his father's sweet, girl-next-door caretaker, was there to ease the pain. It was instant attraction—until Sean found out she was named sole heir, and wondered what her motives really were....

THE O'BANYON BROTHERS

On sale August 2007.

SDCNM0707